lso by Nadine Gonzalez

Miami Famous

Scandal in the VIP Suite
Vhat Happens in Miami…

Texas Cattleman's Club

The Rebel's Return
Rivalry at Play

ver more at millsandboon.co.uk.

Nadine Gonzal
contemporary ro
diverse cast of c
Caribbean and L
by profession, sh
Florida, and shar
her Cuban Amer
their son. She ne
but lives on Insta
@_nadinegonzal

For more informa
website, nadine-g

Disco

Oh So Wrong with Mr. Right

NADINE GONZALEZ

MILLS & BOON

First published in Great Britain 2023
by Mills & Boon, an imprint of HarperCollins*Publishers* Ltd,
1 London Bridge Street, London, SE1 9GF

www.harpercollins.co.uk

HarperCollins*Publishers*
Macken House, 39/40 Mayor Street Upper,
Dublin 1, D01 C9W8, Ireland

Large Print edition 2023

Special thanks and acknowledgement are given to Nadine Gonzalez for her contribution to the Texas Cattleman's Club: The Wedding miniseries.

ISBN: 978-0-263-31265-2

06/23

FSC
www.fsc.org
MIX
Paper | Supporting responsible forestry
FSC™ C007454

This book is produced from independently certified FSC™ paper to ensure responsible forest management.
For more information visit www.harpercollins.co.uk/green.

Printed and Bound in the UK using 100% Renewable Electricity at CPI Group (UK) Ltd, Croydon, CR0 4YY

For Ariel

One

Catch. That. Man.

Sasha had him in her sights. She took off, racing through the crowded airport, up an escalator and down a corridor, desperate to catch up with him before the crowd swallowed him up. The likelihood of that happening was slim. He was a striking Black man, taller than most. But he moved quickly, making long strides, smoothly dodging other travelers as he wheeled a smart carry-on suitcase behind him. Sasha was weighed down by her hefty luggage—a month's worth of clothes—and had to shuffle just to keep up. Was this reasonable, hunting down a stranger at an airport? No, but her options were few. She'd just survived an emergency landing on a plane that looked like it had been pieced together by glue and prayers. The idea of camping out at the airport gate, awaiting the next flight out, made her sick. He was her ticket out.

Wait. Where did he go?

Sasha reached an elevator bank. He was nowhere in sight. The acid in her queasy, empty stomach churned. She wanted to scream, but didn't quite have the energy. She gave up, and not just on pursuing him, on life altogether.

Screw this. She'd grab something to eat and sort it out. It had been a dumb idea from the start.

She located the nearest coffee shop on the airport map and steered her suitcase to Hot Cup of Joe, wondering if their breakfast sandwiches were any good. And that's where she found him. He stood at a counter-height table, a Styrofoam cup in one hand, his phone in another, brows drawn as he read.

She walked up to him and dropped her travel bag on a vacant seat.

He glanced up from his phone and their eyes met.

By God, he was gorgeous.

That shouldn't have been her first thought,

but since it was she might as well unpack it. He was good-looking, emphasis on *good*—no bad-boy vibes here. He had warm brown skin, well-drawn features and the clearest brown eyes she'd ever seen. His short-cropped hair gave him classic boy-next-door appeal. Sasha was weary of those. Every girl's first crush, they stole your heart in junior high and carelessly tossed it back before taking off for college.

He raised a brow, questioning.

She straightened up and tossed back a long box braid over her shoulder. "Remember me? We sat on the same flight, same aisle. You might've forgotten, but you helped me store my camera bag in the overhead compartment."

He'd done more than that. When the plane lost altitude and started its tumultuous descent, he'd helped her with her seat belt. She'd rushed back to her seat from the restroom, where she'd gone to have a panic attack—for totally unrelated reasons—and had trouble clicking the parts together because her hands were shaking so much. He reached over and helped her, tugging on the end of the belt to make sure it was secure. To be fair, he'd checked on the elderly gentleman seated in between them, retrieving his glasses that fell off while he hastily adjusted his oxygen mask. Looking back, he was the only one on the whole damn plane who'd kept it together throughout the ordeal, including the pilot.

He set down his phone. "I remember you," he said, his voice low and raspy.

"You have something I need," she blurted out.

His eyes narrowed with suspicion. "Is that right?"

"Yes. A ride." Sasha raised a finger to silence him even though he hadn't uttered a word. "Before you suggest that I rent a car, you should know that I tried. You scored the last one on the lot. How do I know this? I was in line at the rental car when they put up the NO AVAILABILITY sign. You were the last client they served. And, if you're wondering in what world that automatically makes you my driver, the answer is: This one, a world where I'm stranded in the middle of nowhere and you scored the last rental car."

She paused to catch her breath, suddenly lightheaded.

"Are you okay?" he asked.

She wasn't. The emergency-landing trauma was the least of her issues. A tornado of gloom and doom had followed her from California to Georgia, where she'd made a brief stop for work, like an omen. Who was to say she wasn't somehow responsible for bringing down the plane?

He took her hand and pressed two fingers to her inner wrist. Her pulse leaped to his touch. He withdrew. "Wait here. I'll get you a water."

"Coffee, too!" she called after him. "And a biscotti!"

Sasha watched him go, as cool as ever. Nothing she'd said or done had rattled him, even though she was, by her own standards, pretty much unhinged. What must he think of her? In his suede jacket and jeans that fit just so, he was every inch the sophisticated traveler. She, on the other hand, in her leggings and oversized sweatshirt, a pair of massive headphones dangling around her neck, looked as if she were on her way to the library to cram for finals.

He returned and set a short bottle of water and a tall cup of coffee before her. Hot Cup of Joe wasn't fancy—no milk substitutes and no latte art here—but as promised, the coffee was piping hot.

"Thank you."

"You're welcome." He gently placed a caramel brownie on a napkin. "Sorry, no biscotti."

She smiled gratefully. "That's okay."

There was a quiet stillness about him that she liked. It settled her. The coffee helped, too. As a seasoned traveler it was tough to admit that maybe, just maybe, the plane incident had spooked her.

"They're servicing the car," he said. "Once it's ready, I'll take you where you want to go."

Sasha relaxed for the first time that day. This was far easier than she'd anticipated. She didn't have to twist his arm or resort to blackmail.

"Thank you," she repeated.

"Was Royal your final destination, or—"

"Royal is fine," she said. "Drop me off at the county line. I'll take it from there."

He offered her an easy smile that killed any remaining apprehension. "I'll take you home."

"Royal isn't home," she said, quickly dispelling that notion.

"Where is home?"

His phone buzzed with a text message before she had a chance to answer. He read it and pocketed the phone. "They're ready for us."

Us. The little word wormed its way into her

heart. Everything was going to be fine now. She had someone to rely on. Not that she needed a man to serve that purpose. She was independent and self-sufficient 99.9 percent of the time. Today was a fluke. Sadly, if they never met again, he would forever think of her as the woman who couldn't swim her way out of a puddle.

Sasha finished gobbling up the brownie. Hopping to her feet, she reached for her bag. He beat her to it. "I'll take it from here."

Her battered little heart leaped for joy.

Two

You like the wild ones.

Nik received his cousin's text and had every intention of returning fire. Then she showed up with her swinging braids, feline eyes, deep brown skin and brash attitude. *You like the wild ones...* Where was the lie?

Nik slowed down to keep pace with her. "I don't think I caught your name."

"It's Sasha."

"Hi, Sasha. I'm Nik."

"Thanks again for agreeing to this."

"Don't mention it."

At the lot, they were led to the last compact

SUV. Come to think of it, he was lucky to have scored it. Catching a glimmer of sunlight on her long, frayed lashes, he believed his luck was only getting better.

Nik loaded the truck.

"Need help?" she asked.

"No."

She twitched, restless. "I'll drive! It's a long one, around six hours. We can take turns… And before you make a crack about women drivers—"

"Why would I do that?" Nik interrupted. "Is this 1973 or something?"

"I—I don't know," she stammered. "You wouldn't be the first man to—"

Nik shut the trunk. "Do you always do this?"

"Do what?"

"Argue against points no one's made."

Her expression turned sheepish. "Maybe."

Nik leaned against the back of the SUV. "My dad wasn't around when I grew up," he said. "My mother drove my Little League team all over the state of Florida in a rusty minivan. She did it all, changed the flats and jumped the battery. I don't make *cracks* about women drivers."

She nodded. "Understood."

It was his turn to feel sheepish. That got real

deep, real fast. What had possessed him to share so much?

"The offer stands," she said. "We can take turns driving."

"I'll need to catch up on work emails later, so that's fine by me."

"And I won't interrupt," she said. "If you need to take a call, it's no bother. I've got noise-canceling headphones. You won't even know I'm there. I know you need to make it back in time for dinner, so we don't even have to stop for snacks."

It wasn't until he got behind the wheel, finger hovering over the ignition button, that it hit him. "How do you know I need to get to Royal by dinner?"

"Doesn't everyone want to make it home in time for dinner?" she said with a shrug.

He echoed her words. "Royal isn't home."

"Well…we've got that in common."

He waited. They weren't going anywhere until she fessed up. It took a moment, but she relented. "I might've overheard you making plans over the phone. You asked to reschedule a lunch date to dinner."

"Uh-huh." Nik reached for a pair of sunglasses

in his jacket pocket and tossed the jacket in the back seat. "I'm going to ask you a question. Don't get offended."

She let out a nervous laugh. "I can't promise that, but I'll try."

"Are you stalking me, Sasha?"

She met his eyes. "I am," she said, coolly. "Usually I'm more discreet. Today is an off day."

"Oh, really?"

"I'm a photojournalist," she said. "Observing people is what I do. It's my superpower. I catch details others miss."

Now this was interesting. "What else do you think you know about me?"

She flipped her long braids off her shoulder, readying herself for the challenge. "We boarded in Atlanta. But when you stood to help me with my bag, I caught a glimpse of your boarding pass. You're traveling from Florida. You spent most of the flight reading the *Royal Financial Times.* So I figure you're traveling for business. I can't imagine anyone doing that for fun. You're not wearing a ring. I don't think you're single, though. You're the type to be in a long-term stable relationship."

"Very good," he said, impressed. "Batman and

Sherlock Holmes would approve." The last point, however, was news to him.

She raised her pointed chin. "If I'm wrong, tell me."

She had most of it right. No doubt her "superpowers" served her well in her profession, but he was fairly certain he'd spotted her first, well before they'd boarded the plane in Atlanta.

Nik first laid eyes on Sasha at their gate at ATL. In a holding pen full of anxious people, she sat with her headphones, a faraway expression on her heart-shaped face. To the casual observer she was lost in an audiobook or podcast, but he noticed how her cat eyes tracked all the moving parts, how she studied the people around her, taking in every detail. On the plane, when she took her seat at his aisle, he felt her gaze on him, assessing, measuring and pasting together every bit of information she gleaned for some later use.

"You're right about the *RFT*," he said. "No one reads it for fun."

She considered him a while, her expression inscrutable. "Before I forget. I need your full name."

"I'm surprised you don't know it already, along with my PINs and passwords."

She offered him a sweet smile. "It's not for lack of trying. Believe me."

"May I ask what you need it for?"

She held up her phone. "I'm sending your name and a photo of the license plate to my sister."

"Right," he said. "In case *I* turn out to be a deranged stalker."

"Do you think I'd climb into a stranger's car without some kind of plan?" she asked. "Before you call me paranoid—"

"I would never," he said. "Do me a favor and tell your sister I didn't lure you in with the promise of candy. You *asked* for this ride."

"The eye candy comes standard?"

Nik could not control his smile. "Is that your way of saying you like me?"

She slid him a glance, her expression sour. "Name, please."

"Nikolai Williams."

"Nikolai… Like Gogol?"

"Yes, but call me Nik. Everyone does."

She typed out the text message, attached the photo, and hit send. "Done."

When she looked up from her phone, she was

decidedly calmer. "Listen," she said. "In my heart of hearts, I know you're a perfectly kind, loving and trustworthy human being. In this crazy world, you can't be too careful. You know?"

"I know it," Nik said. "Only wondering who I should text about the woman who carjacked me."

"Your girlfriend, maybe?" she suggested. "That sounds like a good place to start."

She was fishing. Having already figured out that he wasn't married, she wanted to know if he was single. That boded well for him, but he wasn't going to make it easy on her. She'd have to use her detective skills and find out.

"I'll take my chances," he said.

"Let's both focus on arriving in Royal in good spirits and good health," she said. "Sounds good?"

"Sounds great," he said. "I'd like to add one last thing, if you don't mind."

"Let's hear it." She rummaged in her bag for lip balm and dabbed it on her full lips with the tip of her finger. "No murder podcasts? No singalongs?"

"No to that," he said. "But do you remember when you asked me to help you with your luggage on the plane?"

"I'm recovering from a shoulder injury," she said. "It's hard for me to reach. Usually, I manage just fine."

"That's not my point, Sasha," Nik said. "Do you remember what you told me?"

She shrugged. "I don't know. *A little help, please?*"

"No," he said. "*Help me with this and I'll never ask you for anything ever again.*"

"Okay…" she said. "That tracks, but how was I to know the plane was going to plunge out of the sky from cruising altitude—"

"Sasha, that's *not* my point!"

"Well, what is?" she demanded.

"For the next six hours, it's just you and me in this car," Nik said. "I want you to be comfortable. I want you to feel safe. If you need something, if you want anything, even to stop for snacks or just to stretch, tell me. Ask for what you want. You don't have to barter or make promises we both know you can't keep. Just ask. The answer will be yes. Understood?"

Nik was pressed for time. This quick trip to Miami to finalize the sale of his condo wasn't supposed to interfere with that. He'd assured his business partner that he'd be back in time to meet a new client for lunch at the local country club. He hadn't counted on insane travel delays, a plane losing fuel midair and an emergency landing. He hadn't counted on Sasha strutting into his life and making demands on his time. But that's the hand he'd been dealt, and he'd play it.

Sasha fell silent. She looked at him, as if for the first time. Then a devilish glint lit up her eyes. "Careful," she said. "I'll ask for the moon."

"Go ahead," Nik said, and fired up the ignition. "I'll find a way to get it for you."

Three

Headphones on, Sasha stared at the narrow strip of road ahead. To one side of the road there was nothing but amber waves of grain as far as the eye could see. Was there time to stop to snap a few photos? She wouldn't ask. That would be inconsiderate on her part. He had to get back in time for that dinner meeting…no, dinner date? He was so tight-lipped about it. One thing was certain: Nikolai Williams wasn't the mild-mannered boy next door she'd made him out to be. That calm demeanor was steel. When he held her steady in his gaze, she fell to pieces inside.

She fidgeted now, restless, and tugged off the headphones. "The airline better reimburse us," she said. "I used travel points for this trip," she went on. "I'll need them back to book a vacation when all this is over."

"Where will you go?" he asked.

"Anywhere with a nice, calm beach."

"God, I'd like that."

His voice was raspy with yearning. Sasha pushed down the urge to give him all the things he wanted and would not ask for. She could take him away, get him to unplug, push him onto a bed of soft sand and force him to relax. Maybe his girlfriend could do that, if he had one. Why couldn't he confirm if he was single or not? Not that it mattered. In fact, her therapist suggested she swear off men altogether until she sorted some things out.

She deleted the image of Nik wearing close to nothing on a sandy beach. "If not the beach, somewhere fun."

"Royal is fun."

Sasha tossed him a quizzical look. "Is it, though?"

"I might not be the one to ask," he said. "I've only been there for work. Everyone else looks like they're having a great time."

Ever the reporter, Sasha resumed questioning

him. "Where do you live? What kind of work do you do?"

"I'm from Florida," he said. "For the last ten years, I've lived in Miami. I just sold my place because I'm rarely there. And I'm in marketing."

Marketing…of course.

"Is Miami just one big ad agency?" she asked. "Because I'm starting to wonder."

When he smiled or even smirked, as he was now, at anything she said, Sasha felt such a sense of accomplishment. It was ridiculous.

"Okay," he said. "Tell me about your groundbreaking journalism."

"As I mentioned earlier, I'm a photojournalist." She pointed to the duffel bag in the back seat. "That's my gear."

"What are your subjects?"

"My last job was in Georgia. I photographed the aftermath of a flood."

The ring of a phone cut her off. It was coming from the back seat. Nik cursed under his breath, and mumbled something about forgetting to pair his phone with the car's Bluetooth.

"Want me to get it?" she asked.

He responded with a frown. "It's probably not important."

The phone kept ringing.

"Then why are you twitching?" she asked.

"I'm not."

The corner of his eye was definitely twitching. The phone stopped ringing, and started right back again. Sasha could see that it was torturing him. "I'm getting it."

Sasha had released her seat belt and crawled over the center console.

"What are you doing?" he cried. "Be careful!"

"It's fine!"

The ringing was coming from his jacket. She patted the pockets and found it. The ringing stopped just as she pulled it out. She read the screen. "You have two missed calls from someone named Oliver, and a text message from Krystal saying…" She blinked. "Saying you like wild women and it's no wonder you don't have a date—"

Nik circled an arm around her waist, and slammed hard on the brakes. Next thing, they were plunging nose first into a roadside ditch.

Sasha had landed on Nik's lap. She clung to him, breathing erratically. One minute they were driving smoothly, the next they were careening off the road. She grabbed his face between her hands. "Are you breathing? Are you okay?"

Nik gathered her close. "Don't worry about me. Are you hurt?"

There was such genuine concern in his eyes, his voice, his touch, she couldn't help but wrap her arms around his neck, almost choking the man to death. "I'm fine. What just happened?"

"I got distracted, and then a deer jumped out of nowhere."

"No way!" Sasha cried. "Is she hurt?"

He brushed her hair away from her face. "She's alright. Bambi lives to cause another accident."

"What?" Sasha pulled back and searched his face. He was serious as ever. She started shaking with laughter. "Oh God," she said, laughing. "You have a dark sense of humor."

"Don't laugh," he said. "This is my fault. A few missed calls from my business partner wasn't worth putting you in danger."

In the static of her brain, the text message resurfaced. *You like wild women.* What was that about?

"You ignored the calls," she reminded him. "I'm the one who couldn't let it go. Plus, let's not minimize the role Bambi played in this."

He gave her a reluctant smile. “You’re right. Bambi’s the wild card.”

Sasha eased off of him and immediately missed his warmth. “This might be a good time for me to tell you that I’m cursed.”

He looked at her closely. “Want to repeat that?”

“I’m cursed,” she repeated. “It’s probably my fault our plane crashed.”

“Our plane didn’t crash,” he pointed out. “It lost fuel, and landed.”

“We went plunging—”

“It *was* a little rough.”

A little rough? Her heart was in her throat the whole time. “How are you so calm about it?”

“I was in the Air Force.”

“Wait.” Sasha sat kneeling on the passenger seat, hands planted on her knees. “You’re a fighter pilot?”

Nik was staring back at her in bewilderment. “You hear what you want to hear, don’t you?”

“You said—”

“I enlisted straight after high school, and mostly worked in tech. I do fly, though.”

Before she could stop herself, Sasha blurted, “God, you’re hot.”

A bashful expression replaced the bemusement. Sasha revised her opinion. He was hot, smart and brave, but also a little shy about it. She went on teasing him.

"What do I care about airline points? You can fly me to paradise."

He brushed her braids out of the way to take a good look at her. "Sasha, did you hit your head?"

His fingertips skimmed down the sides of her face. In his eyes, she saw genuine concern for her well-being. She had trusted him from the start. Her trust hardened and solidified to something concrete that she could rest on. "Should we get out of here?" she said. "What if we sink into quicksand?"

"Doubtful," he said. "At the very least we should assess the damage."

The SUV was at a slant, leaning heavily on her side. "I don't think I can open my door."

Nik pushed open the door on the driver's side. He got out first and helped her follow him. Nik assessed the damage to the car, which was minimal except for one of the tires that definitely looked flat. They would have to get it towed.

A pickup truck slowed to a stop at the side of the ride. A woman wearing a floppy sun-hat hopped out. “Hey, you two!” she called out. “Y’all okay?”

“We’re fine!” Sasha called back. “Men drivers… Am I right?”

Four

Their Good Samaritan's name was Donna. She co-owned a barbecue shack down the road where they could wait comfortably for the tow truck. Nik loaded their bags into the back of Donna's pickup and turned to Sasha. She stood in the shade, looking uncomfortable.

"Are you alright?" he asked.

"Don't mind me." She fanned her face with her hands. "I'm having a heatstroke."

On the plane her heavy sweatshirt might have been a good idea, but it had now turned into a very effective torture device. "Do you want to change out of that? I'll get your suitcase."

"That's not necessary," she said. "The trick is to wear layers."

She slipped the sweatshirt over her head. Underneath she wore a simple stretchy tank top that clung to her curves. *Nice trick*, he thought and turned away. It was no use. The image of her rounded shoulders and full breasts was seared in his mind.

To distract himself, he pulled out the phone that had put them in this tight spot. Two missed calls from Oliver and a follow-up text.

Client can't make dinner meeting. Lunch is scheduled for tomorrow instead. Same time and place. There's no reason to rush. Take your time and enjoy the drive.

Oliver, who knew him well, had gone out of his way to encourage him to relax. His cousin, Krystal, in her own way, was doing the same. "Your work hard, play hard approach to life is killing you," she'd scolded him. He'd had the not-so-bright idea of stopping by her place to pick up his tuxedo while she was home, instead of waiting until she was at work. The Realtor had staged his condo to look appealing to buyers. Most of his clothes and clutter was stored in Krystal's spare bedroom closet. She'd eyed the garment bag with suspicion.

"What do you need a tux for?" she asked.

"A wedding in Royal."

"Ooh," she cooed. "A *royal* wedding?"

"Might as well be," he said. "Ariana Ramos and Xavier Noble are getting married in June."

"Shut up!" Krystal had leaped into the air like she used to when they were kids. "You're invited to that wedding?"

"Anyone who's anyone is invited," he said coolly.

"Lucky bastard," she said, grinning. "Who are you taking?"

"Would you like to be my date?"

"Sweet of you to offer, baby cousin, but I'll be in Italy perfecting a charcoal sketch of the statue of David by then."

Nik was younger by one year, yet she insisted on calling him "baby cousin."

"Cool," he said. "Suit yourself."

"You mean you can't get a date for one of the most talked-about events of the year?" she asked. "Where are all the women you date?"

"I live here, but I'm constantly on the West

Coast trying to build Nexus," Nik said. "The wedding is in Texas. Try to connect the dots."

"Listen, smart-ass," Krystal retorted. "Women have traveled for way, way less. I once hopped on a plane to attend an indie band's show at a dive bar in Austin with a guy I didn't even like."

"That says more about you than anything else," Nik replied.

"You don't have a date because there's no one you can reach out to, is there?" Krystal said. "You like the wild ones. Trust me, I get the appeal, but those fiery relationships burn out quick. When you're sick, or lonely, or just want someone to talk to, they're no place to be found."

"I'm not sick or lonely," he said. "And I've got you to talk to."

She looked at him disapprovingly. "It's five p.m. somewhere. Let's go to my favorite spot and get margaritas."

Nik checked his watch. "It's five p.m. here."

She waved her hand dismissively. "Let's go. We've got a lot to talk about."

They'd spent the afternoon drinking and talking. Apparently, it wasn't enough, because Krystal had felt the need to follow up with the text message that Sasha had found and read aloud, distracting him to the point that he'd driven into a ditch. Okay, the deer was also to blame. Nik was an excellent driver. He'd never had an accident in his life.

Sasha approached him. "Was the missed call important?"

"No," he said. "Oliver is my business partner. He was calling to let me know that tonight's dinner was canceled. There's nothing to rush back to."

"Nothing?" she said.

"Not a thing," Nik said. "I'm all yours."

She grinned. "You better feed me, then. I've no other use for you."

"Y'all hungry?" Donna said. "You're in luck. Our pulled pork sandwiches are a favorite around here and today's special is boneless ribs with our signature sauce, your choice of tater tots, potato salad or fries, and freshly made churro sticks for dessert."

"Donna, don't tempt me!" Sasha wailed. "It all sounds so good!"

She turned to him. "How about you? Any preferences?"

"I eat everything," Nik said.

"That's what I like to hear," Donna said. "Hope

you two don't mind squeezing in next to me. There's no back seat to speak of."

"We don't mind," Sasha replied. "And we're grateful for your help."

Nik held the passenger door open for Sasha. He climbed in after her. They were packed in so tight, she was practically back on his lap.

Donna got behind the wheel and focused on her driving. Meanwhile Nik couldn't tear his gaze away from Sasha. He liked how friendly and easygoing she was, even after all they'd been through. He wanted to turn things around, make the day better for her. If staying for delicious food was what she wanted, that was what they'd do.

"So let me get this straight," Nik said, once they were seated at a picnic table with sandwiches and a pitcher of ice tea. "You've got superpowers, but you're also cursed."

Sasha popped a tater tot in her mouth and winked at him. Warmth spread in his chest. *You like the wild ones.*

"How does that work exactly?" he asked.

"Let's not go there," she said. "It's such a nice

day. How about you tell me about the wild things you're into? What was that about?"

"Wild cats," he said wryly. "They're harder to domesticate than you think."

He'd expected her to bring up the text message, but he wasn't ready to talk about that.

"That's fair," she said. "Let's stick to simpler topics."

"Okay." Nik switched subjects. "Are you traveling to Royal for work?"

"For a wedding." She licked barbecue sauce off her fingertips. "My sister is getting married. Of all the places in the world, she chose Royal. So I'll be camping out there for a few weeks to hang out with her a bit, keep her sane, and get to know my future brother-in-law better."

"Your sister?" Nik leaned closer to study her. Those eyes, sharp cheekbones and smile… How had he not seen the resemblance before? "Sasha, are you Ariana Ramos's sister?"

She winced. "Should I have mentioned that earlier?"

"And that's the sister you sent my information to?"

"I only have one sister, Nik."

"She probably has me on a FBI watch list by now."

"If it makes you feel better, the text never went through," she said. "I checked earlier, and my phone was still in airplane mode."

"Your future brother-in-law is Xavier Noble," he said. "And I nearly killed you! You're precious cargo, Sasha. I have to get you there safely."

"I'm precious no matter who I'm related to," she said.

"You are to me," he said. "But I've got to deliver you safely to the official Royal wedding committee or they'll run me out of town."

"You have a point there," she deadpanned. "I'll put in a good word."

"You're Ariana's sister," he repeated stupidly.

"Calm down," she said. "I'm nowhere as amazing as her. She was discovered at our local mall when hanging out with friends in college. She started acting and now has her own production company. Between you and me, she was born a star."

"But you're the sun." Sasha did not meet his eyes. Was she shy, all of a sudden? He hadn't meant to put her on the spot, but he'd meant every word. Ariana, whom he'd met in passing, was brilliant. But Sasha glowed hot. If he stared at her long enough, he'd catch fire. "Does it ever bother you to have a famous sister?"

"Sometimes," she admitted. "Like when we just want privacy. I'd like nothing more than to meet my older sister for drinks after a long day at work, but it's always a production. We'd have to go somewhere really exclusive to be left alone, and where's the fun in that?"

Nik didn't have siblings. Hanging out with Krystal, catching up over margaritas, was his therapy. It got him through some tough times.

"Other times," she said, "it's useful, a shield, of sorts."

"How so?"

"Well," she said. "Whatever mistakes I make, however badly I mess up, my superstar sister acts like a lightning rod, drawing the attention to herself and away from me. You can't pay for that sort of protection."

"I'll protect you," he said. "So long as I'm around."

"Promises, promises."

She'd brushed him off, but there was that glow again. All he had to do was tell her exactly what he was feeling to get her to light up from her core. It did something to him.

"I'm invited to the wedding," he said. He might as well put it out there.

She perked up. "You are?"

"It's a work thing for me," he said. "My company just took over the PR firm that handles Xavier Noble's press. We met a few times for business and we're invited to the wedding. I don't have to tell you that scoring an invitation is a big, effing deal."

"No, you don't," she said wryly. "It's the Oscars of weddings."

"Are big weddings your thing?" he asked.

Was it his imagination or had she gone pale beneath her warm complexion?

"Definitely not," she said. "I don't think I'll ever marry."

"Really? Why?"

"My job," she said. "I'm on the road a lot and most men expect their wives to be home for dinner by five."

"You need to meet new men."

Her expression was inscrutable. Nik worried that he'd upset her. Those worries broke like clouds when his phone rang and she reached out and placed her palm over the screen. "Thought you were all mine."

Nik instinctively took her hand in his. At the airport, her pulse was racing and she looked out of sorts. Now she was calm, cool and playful. He wanted to believe that he'd done that for her—even though he'd driven her into a ditch.

"I fed you," he said. "What more do you want?"

She withdrew her hand. Nik wouldn't let her get away so easily. "Come on," he said. "I'm listening. Just tell me."

The most devious smile tugged at her lips. Nik resigned himself. There was no use fighting this thing growing inside him. He liked what he liked, and he liked her.

This time he had no trouble ignoring the ringing phone, but just like last time, it drove Sasha crazy. "Answer it!"

Nik took the call. It was the tow truck driver, confirming their location.

"We don't have long," he said, when he got off the phone. "The driver is twenty minutes away."

"That's a shame," she said. "It's so beautiful here."

"Did you want to stick around and take a tour?" he asked.

"Oh, no," she said. "Ari will worry if I don't make it to Royal by tonight. She's got a whole evening planned. Maybe we could come back sometime."

"Maybe," he said, even though he was thinking, *Definitely.*

She reached for her camera bag on the bench next to her. "Do you mind if I take a few photos? I want to remember this place."

"Please. Go ahead."

Hillside Smokehouse was located in a converted barn set in a field with no hills in sight. It looked like something out of a postcard and he could understand why Sasha would want to photograph it. When she pointed the camera lens at him, he was confused.

"Don't move," she said. "I don't want to forget you, either."

Five

The instant she pressed the shutter button, Sasha knew she could fall for this man. Not only was he strong, he was lovely and attentive. No one had asked how she felt about the big, fat Royal wedding. They only expected her to show up with a positive attitude, lines memorized, ready to play her supporting role. No one had suspected the fresh bout of anxiety it induced, but he had tactfully changed the subject. Sasha had discerned something in him then, something rare and precious. She wanted more of him, not less.

She hadn't come to Royal looking to get involved with anyone. Maybe he could be her date for the wedding. She hadn't thought she needed one. As the maid of honor, she was sure to keep be kept busy. The word *maybe* fluttered about her stomach like a caught butterfly, eager to fly free. Should she ask him? No! Hell, no! Not yet, anyway. She was jumping way ahead of herself. Was he even single? The jury was out on that, even though he was a Grade A flirt. And what was she to make of that text message from Krystal… *You like the wild ones…* That could be interpreted in a hundred ways. How artfully he'd dodged her question with that quip about wild cats! It was cute, but she wasn't fooled.

But what if he were single? What if Krystal was a horse breeder or something? It was possible. They were in Texas, after all. Either way, it didn't matter. That was the beauty of a quick fling. She'd be on a plane to San Francisco in a few short weeks, which meant their emotional baggage could stay locked in storage.

He'd left to take care of the car. She took a few photos of the restaurant and chatted with Donna for a bit. She got the history of the place and even a sneak peek at the kitchen. Donna let her take a few pictures, walked her through the process of smoking meat, and gifted her a jar of barbecue sauce. By the time Nik got back, Sasha had enough for a blog post. She'd pitch the story to a magazine or local publication.

"Packed up and ready," Nik said. "Also, it looks like rain. We should get going."

They thanked Donna and said their goodbyes. Just when they stepped off the porch, a fat raindrop fell onto the tip of her nose. Nik had parked the car in the restaurant's lot, but it was still some distance away. He reached for her hand and together they made a run for it. Sasha shrieked all the way.

They were panting when they made it to the SUV, shrieking and laughing, too. He unlocked the doors and they climbed in.

Earlier, Sasha had slipped on her sweatshirt and only had to take it off. The tank top she wore underneath was dry. Nik was not so lucky. He swore under his breath and yanked his wet T-shirt over his head. "Sorry," he mumbled. "Hope you don't mind."

Not unless he minded her watching.

Rain tapped on the roof and rushed down the windshield, blurring the world. All she saw was smooth brown skin, the cut of his muscles, the lines and grooves that all pointed downward.

The T-shirt came off faster than she'd expected and Sasha was caught staring.

Damn it.

Once again in only a few short hours, Nik questioned her with a raised brow. She turned away.

He reached for a bag in the back seat, pulled out a fresh T-shirt and slipped it on. "The answer is yes," he said.

"I don't know what you mean," Sasha said. "What's the question?"

"The one question you've been asking in a hundred little ways."

"In that case, I have a follow-up question. Who's Krystal?"

His soft laugh rippled down her spine. "My bossy, overbearing, older cousin."

Sasha tore her gaze away from the water-stained glass. His brown eyes were alive, swirling with heat and want. That heat radiated through the car, fogged the windows and walled them in. Sasha's pulse kicked up again. She just couldn't stand it a second longer. She reached for him, grabbing fistfuls of the soft cotton tee, and drew him to her. She raised her lips to his and whispered, "That's all I wanted to know."

"You," he said, his voice gritty.

"Kiss me."

He kissed her hard then withdrew, panting, and cupped her face. "If you distract me again and we drive into a ditch again it'll be your fault, Sasha."

"I'm not worried," she said. "It feels like I'm in good hands."

A strong knock on the car window jolted them apart. The rain had thinned to a drizzle and the world sharpened into focus. Donna stood under an umbrella outside her door. She cradled a jar of barbecue sauce. Sasha took a second to compose herself and lowered the window.

"You forgot this!" Donna cried.

"Thanks!" Sasha said. "I would have cried myself to sleep."

"I doubt it," Donna said with a cheeky little grin. "Drive safe, y'all!"

Four and a half hours later, Nik delivered Sasha to her sister's door. Actually, he delivered her to the lobby of the downtown high-rise where she and her fiancé had taken up residence. Rumpled and disheveled, they looked out of place in the sleek interior, but he didn't care. When he was with Sasha, everyone and everything faded. Nothing mattered.

He offered to take her luggage up, but a porter rushed forward and took care of it. Nik felt crazy territorial, as if the younger guy had stolen his job.

The porter called an elevator. Sasha turned to him with a lopsided smile.

"Thank you," she said. "You delivered me safe and sound. The wedding committee will appreciate it, I'm sure."

There was nothing left to do but say goodbye.

On the drive, they'd talked about everything, from favorite movies to ice cream flavors, but they hadn't discussed what would come next.

"I'd like to see you again," he said, shyness creeping into his voice. "Can I get your number?"

Relief transformed her, erasing worry lines he hadn't noticed before. Nik couldn't believe it. Hadn't he made his feelings clear?

Sasha went through her bag and produced a business card. "That's my number. My email, too, should you need it. Really, just text me."

The card read: Sasha A. Ramos, Photojournalist.

Nik pocketed it. "I'll text you so you'll have my number."

"Okay."

The elevator doors slid open. The porter rolled in the trolley. After following him in, she whirled around and blurted, "Ariana sent Xavier away a few days so we could have some sister time. When he gets back, I'm moving to a hotel near the wedding venue. I'll have a lot more time then."

She either couldn't or didn't care to hide her eagerness. "Alright," he said. "And thank you, too."

She stopped the sliding doors with a firm hand. "For what?"

The elevator sensors chimed. The porter said, "Ma'am." Sasha withdrew her hand. A shadow of regret clouded her expression as the doors slowly slid shut.

He'd promised her the moon, but she'd managed to capture the sun and put it in his pocket. And for that he was grateful.

Ariana flung open the door. "Sasha! Finally!"

Sasha was immediately enveloped in a perfumed hug. The feathered trim of her sister's silk pajamas tickled her nose. "Where have you been? Did you get my calls? Why didn't you return them?"

"It's a long story, Ari," Sasha replied with a heavy sigh.

"Poor little sister, what have you been through?"

"The plane lost fuel. We made an emergency landing six hours away."

"How did you get here? You took a bus?"

A bus? Why hadn't she thought of that? Carjacking an unsuspecting marketing executive from Miami seemed like the most reasonable option at the time.

"If it happens again, *please* make an effort to reach me," Ari said. "I was worried."

Ariana's embrace tightened. Sasha let herself be hugged and loved. When she closed her eyes, she could only think of Nik and the look he'd given her just as the elevator doors walled him out. Those brown eyes were so warm with feeling.

"I want to hear all about it." Ari yanked her inside, but urged her to take off her shoes before going any further. "No offense. You look… grimy."

Sasha stepped out of her sneakers. "None taken."

Compared to her sister, she probably looked like she'd crawled out from under a bridge. Ari looked immaculate. A trained actress, she was most at home on movie sets and had a flair for elaborate costumes. With her cropped hair, golden-brown skin and shapely figure, she was comfortable in the role of the rising star poised to marry an American literary icon.

"I'll give you the grand tour later," Ariana said. "This is the main room. It's comfy."

Not the word Sasha would have used. The furnished apartment her sister rented with Xavier for a couple of months before the wedding was minimal and modern. Floor-to-ceiling windows opened the space to a sweeping view. The low furniture took nothing away from it. Large mirrors and crystal vases added extra sparkle and shimmer. This was home for the next few days, until Xavier returned from a fishing trip with his cousin Tripp. Sasha had every intention of enjoying it, like a free spa getaway.

Her sister took her by the hand. "Let's go to your room."

The bedroom was small. The four-poster bed was not. Sasha couldn't wait to dive in. "Take a long, hot shower," Ari said. "The bathroom is to your right. You'll find a robe on the hook behind the door. Slippers are in the closet."

"Great. Thanks."

"Ice cream?"

"Uh...yes, please!"

Dessert before dinner was their way of acting out a childhood fantasy. Growing up, their mother would not let them so much as bite into a chocolate chip cookie before a meal. To this day, the ultimate act of rebellion was to scarf down cake, flan or ice cream before dinner.

Ari squealed. "Go shower, and I'll set up the sundae bar!"

"Yay!"

The long hot shower revived Sasha. She slipped on a plush robe. She found a pair of fuzzy slippers in the generous closet that housed Ari's designer luggage set. She couldn't believe her big sister was still encroaching on her closet space, and not just for accessories. A picture collage on poster board rested against the closet wall. Sasha picked it up and studied it. Cutouts from various bridal magazines painted a picture of a classic old Hollywood glamor wedding.

"That's my original vision board. I forgot it there."

Sasha jumped at the sound of Ari's voice. She'd entered the room without her noticing.

"It's beautiful."

Ari took the board from her. "We kept the color palette. Only we've added touches of blue. The bluebonnet is the Texas state flower. You won't believe the trouble we went through to find accessories to match just right. It's all in the details."

Sasha stepped into the slippers. "You can plan every detail and things still fall apart."

"What did you say?"

Sasha had muttered the words under her breath. Judging by the look on Ari's face, she'd caught every single one.

"Sorry," she said. "I hate weddings. You know that."

Ari looked aggrieved, as if Sasha had declared she hated kittens.

"You don't *hate* weddings," Ari asserted. "You're far too sweet and tenderhearted for that. You're still haunted by your canceled wedding, that's all."

Sasha let out a caustic laugh. "Is that all?"

"You were smart enough to back out of a marriage that would've ended in disaster," Ari said. "Now you're free to find the true love of your life. It's really not that complicated."

"Aren't you even a little scared?" Sasha asked, her voice shaky.

"Of what?" Ari raised a finger. "Don't you dare say that word."

The word exploded from Sasha's chest. "THE CURSE!"

"For the love of God, Sasha!" Ari grabbed her by the sleeve of her robe and dragged her to the bed. They sat side by side, shoulders touching. "There's no curse. No evil witch hexed us. We are *not* the Witches of San Bernardino Valley."

"What about Mom? And Grandma? How do you explain what happened to them?"

Ari's eyes skidded away. Sasha knew she was being unfair. Now wasn't the time to rehash all of this. If only her sister didn't insist on minimizing her experience to a soap opera plot point. There was nothing uncomplicated about a generational curse. Three generations of runaway brides…it boggled the mind.

"Okay," Ari said. "I hear you. It happens a lot in our family, but it ends now. I am not backing out of this wedding. You don't have to worry about that. Xavier is the love of my life."

The love of her life... Sasha wondered how it would feel to love like that, to be so sure, to leap forward and never look back.

"Nothing short of a typhoon could stop me from marrying him." Ari went on with her rant. "And, on the off chance I am visited by the curse, it's your role as the maid of honor to set me straight. Remind me that on the other side of 'I do' my whole life is waiting with that wonderful man."

"Fine!" Sasha cried, eager to drop the topic. "Can we still be witches, though?"

"Sure. Why not?" Ari said with a laugh. "So long as our witchcraft doesn't interfere with my wedding."

Sasha dropped her head on Ari's shoulder. "You're going to be the most beautiful bride Royal has ever seen."

"Damn right!" she cried. "Now let's go eat ice cream!"

Curled up on the couch with bowls of ice cream drowning in chocolate syrup, they were girls again, only in premium loungewear as opposed to matching pajamas sets. Sasha indulged Ari, and let her carry on about the wedding plans, starting with the venue down to the cake and flowers. When they exhausted the topic, they moved on to gossip. Ari's best friend, Dee, who'd flown to Texas ahead of time to lay the groundwork when Ari was stuck filming on location, had fallen for Xavier's cousin, a guy named Tripp.

"Love is in the air!" Ari proclaimed.

"In that case, I'm going to double-mask," Sasha quipped.

"Don't be a grump," Ari said. "When you're ready, you'll find love."

A phone rang from somewhere in the apartment. Ari sprung from the couch. "That's the doorman," she said. "Probably a delivery. I'm expecting loads of packages."

Sasha licked chocolate sauce off the back of her spoon. "You're going to have to find somewhere other than my closet to stash them all."

"You're too pretty to be petty!" Ari sang on her way to answer the phone.

She was back in a flash, eager to get on with her story. "In the beginning, Dee was all… *I don't have time for love. I'm focused on work.* You know how that goes." She mimicked her friend's tone and mannerisms so well Sasha couldn't help but laugh. "Now she's head over heels in love. There's just something about these country boys, you know?"

"With all due respect," Sasha said. "Royal doesn't qualify as 'the country.' Just look at where we are."

"Tripp is a rancher," Ari said. "He makes his living off the land."

"A rancher?" Sasha said. "Is that a real thing?"

Ari pinched her cheek. "Yes, sweetie, it is," she said. "And careful what you say in these parts."

The doorbell rang. Ari sprung off the couch once again. Sasha went to the kitchen and added another scoop of ice cream to her bowl. She desperately needed comfort food.

From the door, she heard Ari cry. "Nik Williams! What are you doing here? This is a surprise. I thought you were the delivery guy."

Sasha dropped her spoon. Nik?

"I have something for Sasha," he said evenly. "I told your doorman I had a delivery."

"How do you know Sasha? Are you friends?"

Ari's voice had stiffened with protectiveness. It was a tone Sasha knew all too well. The overbearing older sister was flexing her strength. She set down her bowl and rushed out to rescue him.

He stood outside the door, keeping a respectful distance. However, he towered over Ariana and was easily able to scan the interior until his molten brown eyes rested on her. Sasha shivered. The memory of their kiss rushed back to her, nearly bowled her over. How could she have tucked it away? The way he'd touched her, tasted her, tangled his fingers in her hair. She nearly cried; it felt so good.

"Let him in," she said.

Ariana turned to face her. "How do you know him? You just got here. *I* barely know him."

Sasha narrowed her eyes at her sister. "You're being very rude."

"I don't mean to be. I'm just confused," Ari said.

"Ariana!" Sasha snapped. "Who died and made you mom? Let the man in."

When Sasha entered junior high and the neighborhood boys started coming around, Ariana had taken it upon herself to protect her virtue. It wasn't cute then, and it wasn't cute now.

Ari moved out of the way. "Please come in."

Nik stepped into the entryway and the whole room filled with warmth. "I'm sorry for interrupting your night."

"Never mind that," Ari said. "You're welcome to stay. Would you like some ice cream?"

"No, thank you," he said.

He was so polite and polished; Sasha wanted to ruffle him up. "You have something for me?"

"I have your phone."

That simple statement triggered Ariana once again. "You lost your phone and didn't notice?"

"Apparently so," Sasha said.

Normally, she was glued to her phone, texting, responding to email inquiries, or updating her portfolio on three social media sites. The fact that she'd gone this long without noticing was a miracle.

He handed over the phone. "I found it on the floor of the car."

Ariana was well on her way to the kitchen when that last bit caught her attention. "What car? I thought you took the bus."

Nik cut Sasha a glance. Sasha took a breath.

"I never said I took the bus. You assumed that I did."

"Oh, yeah?" Ari folded her arms across her chest. "And who let me go right on assuming?"

"I should go," Nik said.

This time, Sasha blocked his exit. "Don't go. Stay for dinner."

Unlike her, Nik hadn't enjoyed the luxury of a shower and a change of clothes. He wore the same rumpled T-shirt that she'd come so close to ripping off at the Hillside Smokehouse parking lot. He had to be exhausted from the drive. In the end, she hadn't been much help.

"Dinner?" he said. "Don't you mean dessert?"

Sasha's mind wandered. Yes, she meant dessert. Stay for the most delicious dessert.

"She means dinner," Ari cut in. "Don't let the ice cream fool you. That's just our weird sister thing. We've got *plenty* of food. I ordered tacos, all kinds. What are your preferences?"

"He eats everything," Sasha said.

Ari went silent for the first time that evening, taking in Sasha with a steady gaze. "*Vamos a la cocina.*"

Great! Now she was being summoned to the kitchen. *"Porque? No hace falta."*

Nik cleared his throat. “Full disclosure: I speak a little Spanish.”

He was from South Florida. There was a chance his Spanish was better than theirs. Ariana and Sasha were multiethnic and racial. Their father was half-Mexican and spoke mostly English at home.

Sasha smiled up at him. “Is there anything you can’t do?”

Nik stifled a laugh, a shy smile spreading across his lips. Sasha wished they were alone.

Ariana granted that wish. She stomped into the kitchen, granting them a moment of privacy. Sasha watched her go. “You’ll like her once you get to know her. She’s going through some weird overprotective sister phase.”

“I don’t think she likes me,” Nik said.

“You’ll just have to charm her, like you charmed me.”

Nik crossed the distance between them in two strides. “Is that what I did?”

“You know exactly what you did.”

He pulled her to him by the tie of her robe and brushed a kiss to her temple. His breath fanned her cheek. Sasha closed her eyes and let the feeling take her. “Stay,” she whispered into his neck.

"Don't go just yet. Stay and have dinner with me and my oddball of a sister."

His grip tightened on the knot of her robe. "I can't. I'm behind on so many things."

Sasha tossed her head back and searched for his eyes. "Because of me?"

"Let's blame the deer," he said.

"Fair enough."

A clamor from the kitchen broke them apart. Sasha adjusted the flap of her robe. "Thanks for returning my phone. I would have noticed it was missing eventually."

"I was halfway across town when I sent you my number, and it started buzzing."

Ariana poked her head out of the kitchen. "Nik, will you have beer or wine?"

"I have to pass," he said, politely.

"Are you sure?" Ari asked. "Xavier bought a case at a local brewery. He says it's the best he's ever had."

"No doubt it is," Nik replied. "May I take a raincheck?"

"Absolutely. You put up with my bratty sister and brought her home safe," Ari said. "I owe you one."

"That was my pleasure," Nik said.

Ariana returned to the kitchen. Sasha could not hold back her smile. “You charmer,” she said, and led him to the couch.

Six

Ariana pounced just as soon as Nik walked out the door. "I want the whole story and don't leave out a thing. Start talking."

Sasha loaded the dishwasher to keep busy and play for time. She had to be as forthcoming as possible, all the while withholding some crucial details. Sasha told her sister the story of how she and Nik had met on the plane and recounted his bravery in the face of danger. She peppered in anecdotes of their impromptu road trip, leaving out the accident, the parking lot kiss and the way he made her shiver just by whispering her name.

"Let's recap," Ari said. "He's handsome, smart, kind, heroic *and* trustworthy."

"He's all those things." Sasha rinsed a handful of utensils and shoved them in the basket. "What are you getting at? Don't you like him?"

It hurt her to her core that her sister, or anyone really, might not see how awesome Nik was.

"I like him fine!" Ari exclaimed. "I liked him well before you showed up. Nexus took over the company that handles Ex's book marketing. He was very impressed with them."

Nexus had a nice ring to it. Sasha would get him to talk more about his work when she saw him next. Right now, she focused on her sister.

"Did you have to be so rude to him?" Sasha demanded.

"Didn't mean to be," Ari said, contrite. "I've lived in Hollywood for too long. Protecting my privacy is key."

Sasha scoffed. "He's not paparazzi!"

"I'll send him a case of beer or a bottle of scotch," Ari said. "Or better yet, let's all go out to dinner when Ex returns. He's a member of the Texas Cattleman's Club. We'll go there—or somewhere else, someplace nice."

Sasha grunted her approval and went back to rinsing dishes.

Ariana folded her hands on the kitchen counter. "Oh my… This is more complicated than I thought."

"Complicated how?" Sasha asked. In her view, there was nothing complicated about the way she and Nik had come together. It was easy and fun.

"You like him," Ari said.

Sasha rinsed their wine glasses. "What's not to like?"

"No.… I mean, you *like* him."

"Sure," she conceded. "Obviously."

"He likes you, too. I can tell."

"I hope so."

"Where do you see things going?" Ari asked.

Sasha dismissed the question with a laugh. "Going? We just met today!"

Ariana jutted her chin, defiant. "I knew how I felt about Xavier the day we met."

"We're not all as brilliant as you," Sasha quipped. "Some of us are a little slow."

"You're the sharpest person I know," Ari said. "You have a plan for everything. I'm sure you've charted the course of this budding relationship."

"There's no course to chart!" Sasha shut the dishwasher door with far more force than the task needed. "I'll be gone in a few weeks."

"Aha!" Ari cried. "I knew it!"

"Knew what?"

“You’re doing it again.”

“I don’t know what you’re talking about.”

Ari’s eyes narrowed. “I think you do.”

Suddenly frightened, Sasha left the kitchen for her bedroom. Ariana hounded her all the way. Sasha threw herself onto her bed. Ariana did the same.

“There’s no getting rid of you, is there?” Sasha wailed.

“Nope! We’re going to have this conversation, like it or not,” Ari said. “You made me your accountability partner for a reason.”

“When did I do that?” Sasha asked.

“The night you called me—in tears—with the list of your therapist’s recommendations.”

Damn it! In a rare moment of candor, she’d called her sister and confided about the issues that had pushed her to seek therapy. Her therapist had some ideas as to why Sasha’s love life had grown stagnant. If she wasn’t in a committed relationship, there was no risk of being looped into marriage. By restricting her dating pool to emotionally unavailable men, she’d eliminated the risk of ever enduring a marriage proposal that she would likely turn down. It was a foolproof plan. Only years and years of this had left her depleted and numb. That night, on the call to her sister, she'd tearfully admitted to feeling lonely.

"Nik is nothing like the guys I've dated," Sasha said.

There was no shortage of tech bros and finance bros in the bay area. Nik had nothing in common with them. He was decent, generous and considerate. He wasn't a "bro" of any kind. He was a man.

"What does it matter what kind of guy he is if you plan to write him off after the wedding."

"He might be okay with it, Ari," Sasha said. "Have you considered that? He's here on business and may not have the time to—"

"You're proving my point," Ari said. "If he's not open to a relationship, and you know this going in, how is this any different from your past relationships? Wasn't the point to break the cycle?"

Sasha sat up and drew her knees to her chest. Ariana was aggravating, irritating, but she was also right. Under normal circumstances, a fling with a handsome stranger at her sister's wedding was no big deal. Her circumstances were far from normal. She'd enrolled in therapy to deal with the aftermath of ending her engagement and being labeled a runaway bride. She had been dealing with her issues in an open and honest way, going so far as to asking her sister to hold her accountable. Once she'd touched ground in Texas, all of that flew out the window. She was willing to toss out the progress she'd made for Nik's easy smile.

Ari tugged on one of her braids. "With all my heart, I want you to be happy, Sasha."

"I *am* happy," Sasha insisted. "You don't have to worry about that. I'm doing great. I love my job. Did you see last month's spread in *New Day*? That was pretty epic."

"It was epic, and I'm proud of you," Ari said. "I'm just as proud of the work you've done to turn your life around. Promise me you won't flush it down the toilet."

Heart sinking, Sasha turned to her brilliant big sister and said, "I promise."

Sasha couldn't sleep that night. She got out of bed and found her therapy journal. She read the first entry.

Dream I

My grandmother's lace veil cascades down the back of my gown. The chapel is full. He waits at the altar. I take a few steps toward him, gripping my bouquet so hard the flower stems crack. Someone bangs out "The Bridal Chorus" on an organ. The groundswell of music carries me along. Step by step, I make it halfway down the aisle, but no further. My feet sink into the red carpet. Panicked, I look around for help. The wedding guests are strangers. I don't recognize a single one. Panicked, I seek the eyes of the man I'm going to marry and devote my life to. His face is a blur.

My instincts tell me to run, and I do.

Organ music, the swish of taffeta and the cries of the assembly combine in one horrible sound. I push past the ushers, out the chapel doors, and stumble down the steps. Outside all is peaceful. The air is fresh and I can breathe freely. I toss the crumbled bouquet and march down the road.

Dream II

It's a scene straight out of a noir film. I'm in a phone booth, the kind that doesn't exist anymore, weeping into the phone. I tell him that I can't go through with it. The life that he wants is nothing like the one I envisioned for myself. I fear that if I marry him, I'll lose me. I apologize over and over again. His voice comes out loud and clear through the phone line. He is angry and hurt. He should've known better than to trust a woman like me.

"What does that mean?" I say.

The line goes dead.

The second dream was closer to the truth.

Sasha was engaged to a hedge fund manager named Terrence Rhodes. Looking back, she barely recognized the girl who'd said yes to a lifetime of sameness. They met in college. He was the clever one, she the moody artist. They went out on a few dates and just kept on dating. After a few months, their circle of friends had labeled them a couple. Sasha didn't mind so much. Although her feelings for Terrance were lukewarm at best, it beat vying for the attention of the frat bros and jocks. She'd never envisioned a future with him and just assumed they'd part ways after graduation. Instead, they stayed together through graduate school. Terrence went on to business school and Sasha earned her MFA. There was nothing wrong with their relationship, but there was nothing right with it, either. They were an image in muted sepia tones, and Sasha craved color. Just when she started to feel restless and mere weeks after sharing her feelings with Terrence, he went ahead and staged a proposal at a party in front of all their friends. What was she to do? Turn him down in front of everyone?

They postponed the wedding for two years to focus on their careers. Terrence's career in finance took off. Hers putted along, which was expected in her field. Soon, Terrence floated the idea that Sasha quit working altogether after. "No one is saying you can't take photos. Set up a blog or whatever. Soon enough we'll have kids and you won't be able to travel as much if at all."

Set up a blog or whatever… Those words lived rent-free in her soul.

It was the beginning of the end. The wedding plans marched forward as Sasha fell back, retreating into a cave of doubts. It wasn't until the day before the wedding—hours before the rehearsal dinner—that she unraveled before her mother, sister and future in-laws. Sasha slumped down to the floor in a pink tulle dress and burst into tears, proving once and for all that Ariana wasn't the only drama queen in the family.

Terrence walked in and took in the scene. The look he gave her continued to haunt Sasha's dreams.

Her mother reassured her that everything would be all right. Her grandmother stroked her back and muttered, "It's like we're cursed."

Sasha put away the journal and checked her phone for the time. There were two texts from Nik, the one with his number and another one she'd missed.

Sorry I couldn't stay. Would love to meet for a drink when you're free.

Sunshine burst through her cloudy thoughts. Nik made everything better and even though a fling was off the table, no law prohibited them from being friends. She had dinner plans with Ari tomorrow night, but could carve out time for a drink or two. She bit back a smile as she typed a reply.

Tomorrow at 7?

It was close to midnight. She didn't expect to hear back until the morning. However, Nik's response came lightning fast. It's a date.

Seven

"It's not a date," she announced, the moment she arrived.

Nik was waiting at the bar of The Silver Saddle, thumbing through messages on his phone while keeping an eye on the door. For a guy who came up in the school of "time is money," sitting idle like this wasn't his style. Yet here he was, and he didn't even mind. He was just so eager to see her again. And here she was, looking exquisite in a black slip dress that skimmed her body and her braids loose on her back.

After spending all of yesterday with Sasha, Nik found the hours apart dragged on. Nik knew her sister would keep her busy and hadn't expected to see her for days. The open invitation for drinks was just to cover his bases. He had finally gotten around to take a shower when her reply came through. His phone got drenched while he typed out his answer. Even if the thing had fizzled and died, it would have been worth it to learn that Sasha was as eager as he was to meet again.

The hostess pointed in his direction and she glided over, eyeliner-rimmed eyes locked on him. Nik rose to attention. He'd seen her in casual clothes and he'd seen her in a bathrobe; this was a different, dangerous woman. And then she said the words: "This is not a date. Got that? We can only be friends."

"Sasha," he said. "Why don't you have a drink before you decide our future."

"Fine."

She eased onto a barstool and perused the cocktail menu, trying and failing to appear calm.

"What's good here?" she asked.

"The Silver Moon," Nik replied. "It's their signature margarita. Fair warning, it's spicy."

She slid him a glance. "I can handle spicy," she said. "I'm not scared."

"Really?" Then what was leaping like a flame in her eyes if not fear?

Nik signaled the bartender and placed the order. "For how long do I have you?"

Her shoulders drooped. "I'm meeting Ariana for dinner at eight."

That sounded about right. He was no expert, but a non-date date had a cap of sixty minutes. "Let's talk."

She crossed her arms and folded within herself. Where was the wild-hearted woman who'd kissed him in a parked car under the pouring rain?

"I like you," she said quietly.

"I like you, too," he said.

"And I know I might've given you mixed signals—"

"Never mind that," he said.

"I'm only here for a few weeks," she said. "Half that time I'll be busy with wedding stuff. What's the point of starting anything?"

The point was to feel the way they'd felt alone in a rental car with the rain crashing around them. Reigniting that flame *was* the point. She had to know that.

"Before you call me flighty, please know that I've given this a lot of thought."

"I wouldn't call you that," he said. "You can change your mind anytime."

Their cocktails arrived. Sasha sought refuge in hers.

Nik watched her and wondered what had changed since last night.

"Hey, Nik!"

A familiar voice called out his name. It was Oliver, and his new girlfriend Jessica. Nik made the introductions. "Jessica, Oliver, this is Sasha Ramos."

The couple exchanged knowing looks. Nik cleared his throat and continued. "Sasha is a talented photojournalist. Her latest work was featured in *New Day*. She's also Ariana Ramos's sister."

"Wait..." Sasha said. "How do you know about the *New Day* feature?"

"It's this thing called Google," Nik replied.

He wasn't going to hide the fact that he'd searched for her work and combed through her online portfolio. She was extremely talented.

"You didn't tell me," she said.

"I didn't have a chance."

"You guys are so cute," Jessica said "How do you two know each other? Are you old friends?"

"New friends," Nik said, as casually as he could. "Sasha is here for the wedding, as you might've guessed. I've offered to show her around, that's all."

Sasha stiffened at his side. Still, she offered Oliver and Jessica a wide smile.

"We met on the plane to Royal."

It was such a deceptively simple explanation, erasing everything they'd been through together.

"Where were you traveling from?" Jessica asked.

"Georgia. I was there on business," Sasha replied. "Oliver, you must be the business partner I've heard so much about."

Oliver let out a stiff laugh. "Depends. What did you hear?"

"Very little," Sasha admitted. "But only good things."

"So, what are you guys up to?" Nik asked in an effort to move things along. He had nothing but love for Oliver, but he didn't have much time with Sasha. The way things were going, who knew if she'd agree to see him again?

"It's date night," Jessica said.

Oliver and Jessica had come a long way, from fake dating (a long story) to established date nights. That was a leap, and yet they'd made it.

"Hey," Oliver said. "Have you heard anything from Mad Dash?"

Mad Dash was a fast-growing store-to-door delivery service seeking to expand in Texas. Their efforts to get a meeting with the CEO were going nowhere.

"Not a word," Nik said.

"God. It's like they're freezing us out."

Jessica stepped between them. "Sasha, these two will talk business all night if we let them."

Sasha laughed. "What should we do? Tackle them?"

It didn't come to that. The hostess arrived and announced their table was ready. Oliver slid an arm around Jessica's waist. "Why don't you two join us? Let's make this a double date."

Nik was quick to answer. "This isn't a date, and Sasha has somewhere to be."

Again, he felt her stiffen.

"Some other time," Jessica said.

They took off to enjoy their date while he and Sasha endured a stretch of silence. "They're nice people," she said, finally.

"They're the best."

A moment later, she checked her phone. "We should go."

Nik settled the tab without argument. "Where are you meeting Ariana?" he said. "I'll take you."

She grabbed him by the arm and steered him out of the restaurant. "I'm not meeting Ariana. She just canceled. A Zoom meeting with her team is running long."

"Want me to take you home?"

She didn't answer, and he took her silence to mean yes. Disappointment drilled through him. Outside it looked like rain yet again. "Wait here," he said. "I'll get my car."

"Stop!"

Nik stopped cold. "Sasha?"

She stood with her arms at her side, palms open. The doorman, the hostess and even a couple who'd exited right after them, tossed quizzical looks her way. She went to him and spoke in a hushed, urgent tone, as fine needles of raindrops wisped past her face.

"I don't want to go home," she said in a hushed voice.

Nik couldn't help it. He cupped her face and

brushed a drop of rain off her cheek with the pad of his thumb. “Tell me what you want.”

“I’m starving,” she said. “I want dinner, and I don’t want to be just friends, not really. It’s just that things are murky right now.”

The ache of disappointment dulled. He took the first deep breath in a while. “Sasha, one thing at a time. If you’re hungry and want to stay, we’ll stay.”

“No,” she said, firmly. “Take me somewhere quiet. We still need to talk.”

“Okay,” he said. “All you had to do was ask.”

Eight

Nik brought her to Royal Diner, breakfast for dinner. They sat at a cozy booth with stacks of pancakes and butter melting on toast. For dessert, they had a choice of cherry or apple pie. The aroma of coffee clung to the air. It was the perfect spot. Sasha felt safe, supported and…still a little out of sorts.

Sasha respected Nik and believed she owed him the truth. On the other hand, she worried he'd see her differently, wouldn't like her as much. It wasn't an irrational fear. Years ago, the truth had cost her most of her friends. To this day, she had very few.

"Look," she said. "I know it's a lot to spring on you. We literally met yesterday."

Nik cut into his pancakes. "Sasha, stop thinking so much. Tell me what's bothering you."

The words were right there, stuck in her throat that had gone dry just watching him handle his utensils. He had beautiful hands. Her gaze drifted to his face. His brows were slightly drawn and his jaw was tight. She'd done that to him. She'd stressed him out with her "Let's be friends" speech, and immediately regretted it.

His eyes cut to her face. "Sasha, just talk to me."

She picked up her fork and twirled it. There was no other way to go about it except to jump right in. "I'm in therapy."

"That's interesting," he said. "I'm in therapy, too."

She dropped the fork. "You are?"

"No, not really," he conceded. "My therapist is my cousin. Most of our therapy sessions occur over margaritas."

Did happy hour with his cousin count as therapy? Wait… "Your cousin Krystal?"

Something moved behind his eyes. "Dr. Krystal Ann Williams," he said. "She provides counseling for athletes."

Sasha's therapist was a licensed professional who specialized in trauma with whom she met biweekly via live chat, and not a bar. But who was she to judge? To each their own.

"What do you talk to her about?"

"Let's focus on you."

It was too late for that. Curiosity was nibbling at her everywhere. He was so self-possessed. She couldn't imagine anything unraveling him. "I need to know, Nik. Tell me your demons."

"Alright," he said. "I'm invited to your sister's wedding."

That explained nothing. "Pretty sure most of Royal is."

"I don't have a date, and that's fine," he said. "Krystal pointed out, over margaritas, that my relationships don't stand the test of time."

"Because you like the *wild* ones."

"*I* like the wild ones."

He looked her dead in the eyes, sending a shiver racing down her spine.

If he thought she fell into that category, he was in for bitter disappointment. She wasn't the wild girl, or the party girl, or the girl who lived off coffee fumes and crept home at 3:00 a.m. Work-related travel aside, she lived a sedentary life… for a witch.

Sasha slathered even more butter on her toast. "Tell me about these wild women."

A hint of a smile lit up his gorgeous face. "I'm not a lion-tamer, Sasha. The last woman I dated worked in luxury retail. She moved to London for a promotion. She now works at the flagship store. She chased her dream. There's nothing outrageous about that."

"You didn't chase after her?"

"No," he said. "I chase my own dreams."

Those words landed with a thump in her gut. Nik wouldn't chase anyone. If she, or anyone, really, it didn't have to be her, ran away, he'd let them go.

"Last summer, I met Tracie, a forensic accountant. She *was* wild, but she was fun."

Sasha reached for the syrup. "I bet."

"Now tell me your demons, Sasha," he whispered. "I need to know."

"I am what they call a runaway bride," she said easily. When he said her name like that, she'd confess to arson.

He stopped and considered her words. She

watched the internal debate play out. "You were engaged before?"

"Yes."

"It didn't work out."

"Accurate."

"You…ran out of the chapel or whatever."

"I called off the wedding the night before," she said. "There was no dramatic music."

"You changed your mind."

"Yes, but it's not as simple as that."

He dunked a forkful of pancakes into a shallow puddle of syrup. Sasha couldn't touch her food. Her appetite was gone.

"Did you love him?" he asked.

"Not enough, apparently," she replied. "I was twenty-five, and wanted to chase my own dreams, too."

"Everyone deserves the chance," he said. "Do you feel guilty about that?"

There was plenty to feel guilty about. She'd hurt Terrence, humiliated his family, disappointed her friends, and had a hand in perpetuating a family curse.

"It's not as simple as that, Nik."

"You keep saying that, but I don't see it," he said. "Twenty-five is young. Most people aren't ready for marriage. You're allowed to change your mind, Sasha. I get the timing wasn't ideal."

"I'm not the first person in my family to have changed my mind. I'm not even the second."

He paused at that. "Really?"

"My mother and grandmother both canceled their engagements."

It was a long story, so she dove right in. She told him how her grandmother had quietly ended her engagement to her neighbor's son. It wasn't a great scandal. She returned the ring and it was never spoken of again. Her grandmother called it a "false start."

With her mother, things didn't go so well. She jilted a handsome young doctor, left him standing at the altar, the sin of sins. The community uproar was deafening. She paid a high price for that act of bravery. Sasha's grandmother understood and supported her decision. At the time, her grandfather could not bear the sting of humiliation. He did not yell or threaten. He gave her the silent treatment, instead. He even went so far as cutting her off financially to "make up for the expenses of the wedding." It became too much for her mother to bear. She fled her small town and relocated to San Bernardino.

"It's a pattern," he said. "Is that why you're in therapy? To understand the pattern."

When he put it that way it sounded so logical. She had to set the record straight. "It's not a pattern, Nik. It's a curse, a family curse."

Nik pushed back his plate. "We need coffee."

Sasha took a bite of toast and waited for Nik to return from the counter with their drinks, certain he would never take her seriously again.

"I have questions," he said.

Sasha expected as much. She wrapped her hands around her coffee mug just to warm her hands. "Go ahead."

"If it's a curse we're talking about, do you need a therapist or some other kind of professional?"

"Nik."

"What about Ariana? Will she go through with this wedding, or are you worried about that?"

"My sister will marry Xavier come hell or high water," Sasha said. "She's the exception that proves the rule."

Nik took a sip of coffee as he tried to puzzle it out. Far from clearing things up, she'd muddied the already murky waters. "You're confused. I shouldn't have said anything."

"I am confused," he said slowly. "I'm wondering what, if anything, this has to do with you and me."

"I…uh…my therapist thinks I've developed an avoidant trait when it comes to relationships. I've been doing the 'no strings attached' thing for a while now as a way of avoiding… See, if you're not anyone's girlfriend, odds are you'll never be anyone's fiancée."

"That's one way to go about it," he said.

"It's tiresome in the long run, holding people at arm's length," she said. "It's lonely."

She'd dated some pretty nice guys. Having always to pretend that she was too busy with work to commit to a relationship, always being the one to disappoint the other, it eroded her heart. She wasn't that person.

"I can see how it would be," Nik said.

"You're big on patterns. My therapist recommends I break the pattern."

Sasha stirred sugar in her coffee, folded her napkin, and wondered aloud if it were time to ask for the check, anything to avoid Nik's eyes.

"What about cherry pie?" he said.

"Did we agree to that?" Sasha asked. "I was leaning toward apple."

"We'll get both."

"Good call." Sasha scanned the sleepy diner for the waitress.

"Sasha, look at me."

She shook her head. "I can't."

"Okay, don't." He rested his hand, palm up, on the table. "Put your hand in mine."

It took a while before she placed her trembling hand in his. His fingers folded around hers. Sasha let out a jagged laugh. "You think I'm ridiculous, don't you?"

"I don't."

"I wouldn't blame you if you did."

"Want to know what I think?"

Sasha finally looked at him. She searched his face for judgment and ridicule and was relieved to find no trace of either.

"I think you've been through some things," he said. "I'm no therapist, but I imagine your sister's wedding is wildly triggering. So, how about we split some pie and be friends?"

Sasha welcomed his words with a smile, even though nothing felt quite right.

Nine

Ariana invaded at dawn. She bolted into the bedroom without so much as a courtesy knock. "Wake up!"

Sasha roused from sleep with a start. "Ari! Seriously?"

"Sorry! You have to see this video."

Sasha groaned and buried her face in a pillow. "It's five o'clock in the morning. Unless someone we love is breaking a world's record of some kind I don't want to see it."

"It's ten thirty," Ariana shot back. "I've done Pilates and made scrambled eggs."

Sasha looked up and around in a stunned stupor? "Ten thirty in the *morning*? How?"

Her sister grabbed a remote control off the bedside table. "It's the blackout drapes. I told you, they're amazing."

With a push of a button, the drapes parted to reveal a splendid midmorning sky. Sasha could only peer at it through the web of interlaced fingers. The pristine light was blinding. "I haven't slept so well in years."

"It's this bed. I told you, it's amazing."

Ari went on about the bedding. Sasha doubted the down-filled pillows or Belgian linen sheets had anything to do with it. Her conversation with Nik last night had left her feeling light and unburdened like never before. That feeling had stayed with her. She hadn't slept so soundly or felt this clearheaded in years.

She stretched and yawned. "Okay, I'm up! What's this video about?"

"A wedding crasher."

"Ari, the wedding is weeks away. A wedding crasher doesn't announce itself."

"Well, this one does," she said stubbornly. "Have you heard of Trick MacArthur?"

"Trick who?"

"He's a professional wedding crasher," Ari replied. "He stalks celebrities and finds out as much as he can about their wedding plans and leaks the information on social media. He's been seen poking around Royal and it's driving my wedding planner crazy."

Sasha couldn't believe it. "You mean to tell me there's a grown man out there crashing weddings just for kicks?"

"Not just any wedding!" Ari exclaimed. "*Celebrity* weddings."

Sasha looked up to the vaulted ceiling. "Excuse me. I misspoke."

"He's not doing it for fun, either," Ari said. "He's doing it for money. His videos consistently go viral." Ari climbed onto the bed and thrust her phone in Sasha's face. "Look what he's posted to his stories this morning!"

A video was cued up. Sasha hit play.

A guy with thick brown hair and friendly eyes grinned and waved hello. "Hey, all! Good morning from Texas!"

All told, he looked harmless enough. Handsome, too.

"I'm at this charming little bakery in Royal, Texas," he went on. "My sources say the Noble-Ramos wedding planner has been spotted ducking in and out of this establishment. Should the couple order their wedding cake from here, I have a few suggestions. According to the head baker, Funfetti is the most popular flavor. Can you imagine Ariana Ramos going for anything as *fun* as that? Me, neither! If it were up to me, I'd go with either chocolate raspberry or chocolate cappuccino. Both are excellent flavors, but then again I got a thing for chocolate. Who knows what the actress will pick in the end. So long as they don't go for plain old vanilla! Signing off now. Don't forget to like, subscribe and all the things."

Sasha hit Pause. Silence settled in the sun-filled bedroom. She turned to Ari, curled up beside her. "You're going with plain old vanilla, aren't you?"

"Xavier's grandmother is allergic to chocolate!" Ari wailed. "We went with a Tahitian vanilla laced with bourbon from a local distillery."

Sasha stifled a laugh. "Sounds delicious."

Ariana grabbed a pillow and curled into a fetal position. "I like funfetti just as much as anyone! How dare he suggest I don't?"

"The audacity!" Sasha chimed.

"Our cake will be covered in bluebonnet flowers made of sugar in honor of Texas!"

"See? Shows what he knows."

"Do you think we should add an extra Funfetti cake…for the kids?"

"No, I don't." Sasha rubbed her sister's back. "And you don't have to justify your choices to this trickster."

"He won't stop at the cake," Ari said. "Nothing is off limits. He leaked photos of Chelsea Carlisle's bridesmaid dresses and revealed her song choice for the father-daughter dance."

"How did he know?" Sasha asked. "Did he hack the DJ's computer?"

"How would I know?" Ari wailed. "He's dangerous!"

"Calm down, Ariana. You're overreacting."

"Easy for you to say! I'm freaking out. Rylee is stressed out."

"Who's Rylee?"

"My wedding planner!" Ari snapped. "She's excellent!"

"Oh, right…" Sasha collected her sister in her arms. "Don't freak out. I can see how this is aggravating. I totally understand."

"What should I do?" Ari asked.

It wasn't every day that your older, wiser and

more fabulous sister asked for advice. Sasha was at a loss. "What did Chelsea Carlisle do?"

"Nothing."

"That's probably all you can do," Sasha said. "If you go for a restraining order or anything like that, you'll end up generating more publicity for him."

"That's what Xavier said," Ari said quietly.

"Listen to me," Sasha said. "When did we start caring about what random people think of us? We are the Witches of San Bernardino Valley, remember? We're no strangers to a little wedding drama."

"You're right," Ari said with grim determination. "Our grandmother didn't buckle, our mother faced it head-on, and you thrived."

"I wouldn't go that far," Sasha said, interrupting. "I'm barely holding it together."

"False," her sister said. "You're radiant, confident and successful."

"Ari, I'm in therapy for a reason."

"The reason being that you're self-aware enough to analyze your issues instead of burying them."

"When you put it that way, it doesn't sound so bad."

"You're on the right track, Sasha. Believe in yourself." Ari pulled away from her. "Now tell me the truth. Do you think my cake is boring?"

"Are you kidding?" Sasha said. "If I don't get a sugar bluebonnet on my plate I'm going to have a fit. And Trick can choke on it!"

Ari cuddled closer. "I'm so glad you're finally here. You keep me grounded."

"And you keep me sane," Sasha said. "We'll get through this together."

Ari sniffled. "Hug me tighter."

Sasha laughed. "Whatever you need."

Her sister tugged on one of her braids. "Sorry I skipped out on dinner last night."

"Don't worry about it. It's fine."

"I'll make it up to you. Tonight we're going to a cocktail party at the Cattleman's Club."

"That's how you plan on making it up to me? By dragging me to a cocktail party? You know I hate those things."

"Come on, Sasha. It's for a good cause, and I can't get out of it," Ari pleaded. "We won't stay long. I promise. A half hour tops. Then we'll duck out to the club's wine bar and hang out. It'll be fun."

"You mean, Funfetti?"

"Ha ha!" Ari droned. "What will you wear to the party?"

Sasha responded with a lazy one-shoulder shrug. "A little black dress. I packed a few of those."

Ari frowned. "That won't work."

"Don't be ridiculous. A little black dress always works."

"There's a dress code. We're supposed to wear white."

"Now you're just screwing with me!"

"Didn't you pack a little white dress?" she asked sweetly.

"No, Ariana. I didn't," Sasha said. "Do you know why? I was packing for a wedding. I figured I'd let the bride shine."

"That's so considerate of you, but you didn't have to take it that far! I'll shine no matter what."

"I'm sure," Sasha grumbled.

"Don't worry. I have a white sundress you can borrow. It's super sexy."

"Gee, thanks."

Ariana climbed out of the bed. "Now you really have to get up. I made you breakfast and it's getting cold."

She bolted out the door, leaving Sasha to wonder if the wedding was causing her to unravel. Sasha reached for her phone and saw she had two messages from Nik.

Thank you for last night.

Pancakes never tasted so good.

Sasha wiggled her toes under the fine linen sheets. *This* was how she was meant to start her day. She typed a response.

Therapy has never been so effective.

Had she known that a conversation with a friend was all it took to clear the cobwebs of the past, she would have done it ages ago. Sasha felt unburdened as never before. Then again, no one, besides family, had showed the patience and respect that Nik had last night.

Are you warming up to the idea that therapy doesn't have to happen in a clinical setting?

No, that wasn't it. I'm warming up to you.

Three dots popped up and vanished. Sasha's

heart skipped with each second his answer was delayed. She couldn't blame him for being cautious. She was all over the place. One minute she was kissing him in a rental car in the rain. The next she was claiming she only wanted to be friends. *And then* she went and told him that she was cursed. What must he think of her? For his own sake, he should run away screaming.

I want to see you again.

I should give you space, but that's what I want.

While she went on a merry-go-round of madness, he'd sent two clear, concise messages expressing his desires and misgivings. God, this man!

I want to see you, too!

Like now! Like right now!

Do you have plans with Ariana for tonight?

She's dragging me to a cocktail party at a country club.

The three dots of purgatory popped up and vanished once again. And finally, a response: I have something like that on my calendar. Do you have to wear white?

That's the one! Please come.

I'll see what I can do.

Ten

So, this is the world-famous Texas Cattleman's Club... Sasha caught her reflection in one of the gilded mirrors in the club's lobby. In a white fitted halter dress and her braids loose down her bare back, she looked...amazing. Yay for her, but really she was on the lookout for Nik. The mirrors allowed her to go about it as discreetly as possible until they were led out to a terrace overlooking the club's sweeping grounds. She scanned the crowd. Nik wasn't among the beautiful people dressed in white.

"This is fancy," she said to Ariana. "What's this event for again?"

"We're raising awareness for melting polar ice caps."

"Really? Is that what we're doing?"

"*Yes.*"

"Can't you do what I do? Just write a check!"

"It's not enough, Sasha. Sometimes, you have to show up and—"

Ari's speech was cut short. A small crowd gathered and swallowed her up. Everyone wanted to meet the Hollywood actress poised to join Royal's elite. Some wanted her autograph. Others wanted to pitch ideas. Others, still, solicited charitable contributions.

Sasha stood to the side, ignored and unnoticed. A waiter approached. "Champagne, miss?"

"Yes, please." She lifted a flute off the server's tray.

Sasha sipped her champagne and enjoyed the spoils of anonymity. The waiter, however, did not move. "Is there something else?" she asked.

"Mr. Williams requests that you meet him at the bottom of the stairs in ten minutes, if you can."

Sasha brightened. He deserved a tip for that. "Which stairs? Where?"

The waiter pointed to the winding staircase, which, according to him, led to the tropical gardens.

"Thanks!" She slipped him a twenty.

Sasha didn't wear a watch. She kept track of the time on her phone. This was considered rude in most settings, let alone an elegant cocktail party. There was no way to go about it without looking bored and disengaged. She must have caught Ariana's attention because she excused herself from the crowd and shuffled over to Sasha. "Sorry I've abandoned you."

"No worries!" Sasha said lightly. "Do your thing. It's alright."

"It's *not* alright," Ari said. "Come with me."

She gripped Sasha's arm and drew her to the group. "Have you met my sister? She's a talented photojournalist. You might be familiar with her work."

Sasha had no choice but to engage in small talk, even as a countdown clock was ticking off the seconds in her brain. In just a few minutes, she'd see Nik again. She answered a few questions about her work and nodded to show interest in what the others had to say right up until an imaginary alarm went off in her head. *Okay. That's it. Gotta go.*

Ariana was engaged in a discussion with the non-profit organization's treasurer. This was her chance to slip away. She worked her way through the crowd and, heart pounding, heels clicking on the stone tile, raced down the stairs before anyone or anything could stop her. She spotted him at the bottom of the stairs, his back to her, looking stylish in cool tones of gray. Sasha stopped to catch her breath. If she didn't grip the handrail, she'd swoon.

"Hey you!" she called out.

He turned around and took a step back. "Hey gorgeous!"

"You're not observing the dress code. That's a bold move."

He grinned at her. The fading sun tinged his brown skin gold. "Sorry. I don't own white trousers and didn't have time to shop for a pair."

"Is that why you're not coming up?"

"I don't think they'll miss me." He held up a picnic basket. "I tipped a waiter and look what I got. Party of two?"

She rushed down the few remaining steps and into his arms. "Take me away."

He brushed her braids off her shoulder. "I hate to steal you away from your sister. You're here to spend time with her."

But I want to spend time with you.

She slipped her hand in his and tugged him down the brick garden path. "Are you kidding? Ariana has been driving me crazy."

"Is it the wedding?" he asked.

"This time it's a wedding *crasher*."

"What?"

"I'll send you one of his videos," Sasha said. "He's real funny, actually. Just wish he wasn't targeting my sister."

They came across a fountain surrounded by trees. "This'll do," Nik said.

He spread a blanket on a patch of grass. Sasha stretched out on her side and watched him unpack a chilled bottle of sparkling wine and the assortment of appetizers that the catering staff were offering on trays at the party. "Speaking of my sister," she said.

"Yes?" He uncorked the bottle of sparkling wine and carefully poured her a glass.

"She can't know about us."

Nik looked up at her, his beautifully chiseled face frozen in surprise. "Us?"

"She…disapproves." Sasha took the glass from him and sipped. "Ariana wants me to follow through my therapist's recommendations and wait until I'm ready for something real. We had a long talk about it. I don't want to upset her this close to the wedding. She's stressed out enough as is."

"I don't understand." Nik picked a bright red strawberry from a container and brought it to her lips. Sasha bit into the fruit. It was sweet as summer. "We're just friends. What's to approve of?"

"Friends don't look at their friends like that, Mr. Williams."

"You got me there," he said. "I'll do better."

Nik dipped the half-eaten fruit in cream and returned it to her lips. Sasha had a sudden pang of hunger. Her lips parted slightly. She licked the cream before taking a bite. The gurgle of the fountain, the setting sun, the scent of fresh-cut grass, all of it was going to her head. Being here with Nik was an incredible luxury. She did not take it for granted.

"Here's what worries *me*," Sasha said. "I don't have warm, fuzzy, friendly feelings for you. I think about the way we kissed. The memory doesn't go away. It never fades."

Nik went still. "Then come kiss me."

God, she wanted to! Nothing was holding her back except a thread of defiance. "*You* come *here*."

He set aside the bowl of berries from which

he was feeding her and focused on her. "If I kiss you," he said, "I won't want to stop."

Her sharp laugh betrayed her inner turmoil. "There's not much we can do out here in the open. Is it safe?"

"That's not what I mean."

He rested a hand on the rise of her hip. Sasha closed her eyes. The warmth of the sun and the subtler warmth of his hand spread throughout her body.

This put an end to the "let's be friends" debate. Let's *not* be friends, she thought. That was a stupid idea from the start. All she wanted was his body, to know his kiss, and find out what those strong hands could do. These were not warm, fuzzy, friendly thoughts.

Sasha opened her eyes and found him studying her. She drew him to her by the sleeves of his crisp gray shirt. "I know what you mean," she said. "I want you to kiss me anyway."

This was the time for him to press his body on hers and crush her lips with his kiss. He did not do that. He took his time, sliding his hand from her hip to the curve of her breasts. She fit nicely into his palm. His other hand found the tie of the halter dress. “Sasha,” he said. “How committed are you to playing it safe?”

She always felt safe with Nik. They had their own special kind of luck, carrying them through near disasters, accidents and freak storms.

“Not very much,” she admitted.

With one tug of the tie, the knot came undone. She brought her hand to her chest and inched down the fabric, offering herself to his gaze.

“I’ve been wondering and wondering and wondering...” Nik whispered.

“What about?”

“This.”

He swiped the pad of his thumb against a tender nipple. Sasha tensed with frustration. There was too much space between them. She reached up and pulled him close by the nape of his neck. Their kiss was less urgent than their first. This kiss was deep and slow. It sealed a silent pact between them. They could be lovers. They could be friends. Nothing was off limits.

He pulled away and murmured “strawberries” before his mouth slid down her throat and closed on her other aching nipple. Every flick of his tongue brought agony and pleasure. Sasha raked her fingernails down his back. She wanted to claw off his shirt and feel his skin. She would have, too, if not for the sound of footsteps and laughter in the distance.

Nik pressed his chest to hers and hastily fastened the ties to her halter top. The voices faded and the footsteps veered in the opposite direction, yet Sasha clung to Nik, laughing at the thought of getting caught topless in the well-kept gardens of a country club in Royal.

He kissed her shoulder. "I should take you back to the party."

Sasha had a better idea. "You rescued me. Now it's time to rescue my sister."

They plotted to pull Ariana out of the party. It was for her own good, Sasha reasoned. Her sister was intent on stunning the world with her charm, grace and beauty until her star burned out. Someone had to save her from herself.

Nik recruited his inside man. This time the waiter was less accommodating. Throwing together a picnic basket and passing a message on to Sasha, an unknown, was one thing. Interrupting the famous Ariana Ramos while she held court was quite another.

Sasha slid him a twenty-dollar bill. "Tell her

Sasha is asking to speak with her at the lobby. Tell her it's an emergency."

"I can't do that," the young man protested. "I'll lose my job."

"You won't," Sasha said. "I'm her sister. She won't mind."

"With all due respect, ma'am, why not approach her yourself?"

Nik pulled a hundred-dollar bill from his wallet. "With all due respect, will this cover the inconvenience?"

The waiter pocketed the money. "It will. Thanks."

The waiter took off. Sasha inched closer to Nik. Giddy as children, they watched the scene play out from outside the French doors to the terrace. The young man approached the group of six that had tightened around Ariana. He delivered the message. Her eyebrows soared heavenward. Sasha almost felt sorry for her.

Ariana promptly excused herself and exited the terrace. Her white dress had a full skirt and it twirled with each urgent step. Even in a panic, she was graceful and elegant.

"Sasha!" she cried. "Where were you? What's

the emergency?" Her gaze cut to Nik. "Hey! You're here, too!"

"Calm down," Sasha said. "We're breaking you out of here."

"This isn't prison, Sasha!"

Sasha threw her hands up. "It might as well be!"

Ari scolded them in her motherly way. "You two are terrible!" she said. "Nik, you're a serious person. Did Sasha put you up to this?"

Nik bore a serious expression that brought out his high cheekbones and sharp jaw. "She did, actually."

"Nik!" Sasha cried.

"Keep your voice down!" Ari hissed. "This is the TCC."

She said it as if it were the Vatican. "Look, are you coming or not?"

"Of course I'm coming," Ari said. "Let's go."

Eleven

Nik was enjoying dinner in the company of the two most beautiful women in Royal, arguably in the world. He had no complaints.

At Ariana's suggestion, they left the party and walked over to the wine bar on-site. Dinner was simple: burgers, fries and a vintage bottle of wine. Nik sat next to Ariana and across from Sasha. It took everything he had inside to keep from staring at her beautiful heart-shaped face. He hung on Ariana's every word just to prove that he found her just as interesting as her sister, but the truth was in the drumbeat of his heart. If Sasha laughed, which she did often, particularly when she showed him snippets of videos of the "wedding crasher" prowling around Royal, his heart gave chase.

"You have to agree, it's hysterical."

"It's stupid," Ariana retorted through uncontrolled laughter. "And stop watching his content! You're encouraging him."

Love him, hate him, the videos were funny. The guy had a workable concept. Nik would sign him on as a client, if it wouldn't cause them to lose Xavier's account.

The waiter set the dessert menu on the table. Ariana immediately protested. "Just coffee for me," she said. "I have to fit into a dress in a few weeks."

"Sasha, how about you?"

It was the first time he'd uttered her name all night. It felt like a caress on his lips. She looked up at him, beaming. That was the only word for it. She beamed.

"I'm up for pie," she said. "Apple or cherry."

"Or both?" he said. "We'll share."

"Why not?"

"I'll tell you why not," Ari said. "I can't be around so much pie!"

"You have to eat it before it does any harm," Nik said.

"Or any good!" Sasha fired back.

Ariana brought her fingers to her temples. Her diamond engagement ring caught the candlelight and flashed. "You two together are a menace," she said. "Nik, I'm sorry to say, you've let my sister corrupt you."

Even if that were the case, Nik wouldn't mind at all. *Corrupt me all you want, Sasha.*

His phone rang. He recognized the number as his contact over at Mad Dash, the start-up company whose business he was chasing. "If you don't mind, I have to take this. It's business."

This time he spoke directly to Sasha. She responded with a hint of a smile. He knew she was thinking about the last time he'd missed a business call and all the things which had followed.

"We don't mind," Ariana said. "Don't worry. We'll order your pie."

Nik stepped outside. The call had gone to voice mail. He phoned back. Tony Collins, an old college buddy and the director of development at Mad Dash, delivered bad news. "Caroline left for Arizona for three weeks. She's on a wellness retreat and not taking any calls."

Caroline Lewis was the start-up's CEO and founder. Nik needed only a meeting to show her all the ways Nexus could get Mad Dash established in Texas. She'd avoided him at every turn. Nik wasn't one to give up easily, but it was starting to look like he was wasting his time chasing this account. "How many interviews did she take, Tony? Do you know?"

"About three," Tony replied. "I'll tell you the truth. I don't think she's comfortable switching teams right now."

The company had received an influx of cash at its last financing round. Now was the time to expand and grow. "That makes no sense."

"The current head of marketing is her best friend," Tony explained. "That's why she's dragging her feet on this. She might not want to shake things up."

Nik considered this. He wouldn't toss over Oliver for anyone. This was beginning to look like a dead end.

Krystal called just when he got off the call with Tony. "Hey you," she said. "I'm leaving for Italy tomorrow."

"I know. I meant to call you later."

A clinical therapist by day, a self-taught cook by night, Krystal was chasing a lifelong dream. She secured a spot in an art class for the summer. It was expensive and impractical, but she was doing it. He was proud of her.

"Just calling to let you know that I changed my security code in case you want to crash here while I'm gone," she said. "I don't feel comfortable sending it to you in a text message, so here it is." She repeated a five-digit code five times. "Got it?"

"I got it!"

"Good. Write it down somewhere safe."

Krystal lived alone and took her security seriously. He couldn't even blame her. The world was a scary place. "I got it," Nik said. "Anything else? I've got to get back to dinner."

"Nothing at the moment," she said. "Talk soon."

"Hey Krystal!"

"Yes?"

Nik stepped away from the door, even though no one was around. "I've been thinking a lot about what you said. That thing about the type of woman I'm attracted to."

"I'm listening."

"I don't think it's wrong."

He'd been thinking about this a lot. According to Krystal's theory, he'd have to give up excitement and spontaneity for love, happiness and fulfillment. He wasn't prepared to make that exchange. He wanted what he wanted. For now, it looked very much as if he wanted Sasha Ramos.

"There's no right or wrong," Krystal said. "There's just what is. I want you to be clear-eyed about the choices you make."

He was nodding, aware that Krystal couldn't see him.

"Are you there?" she said.

"Yes," he said. "But I gotta go."

"Call me later this week. We'll talk more."

"Sure," he said, although he didn't need to talk much more. He'd already made his choice.

Sasha was alone at the table when he returned. "Why are you alone?" he asked. "Where's Ariana?"

"She's in the ladies' room, and I'm not alone. I've got pie."

She presented the two plates with the grace of a game show host. Nik grabbed a fork. "Your sister doesn't know what she's missing."

"I had a good time tonight," Sasha said. "Thanks for coming."

Her voice was uncharacteristically subdued. Nik set down his fork and looked at her, took in the lines of her face from the gracious arch of her brows to her sharp cupid's bow. In her white dress, she looked like something from a fairy tale. He could not keep his eyes or his hands off her all night.

"Sasha, all I want is to be around you. I want… more of you, all the time. I know it makes no sense." He used his spoon to drive his point. "Before you say that it's too soon—"

She grinned. "I would never say that."

"Good," he said, and drove his spoon into the golden slice of apple pie. "I know my mind."

"'I know my mind'…" She repeated his words in a whisper. "God, I love it when you talk that way, so self-assured, so sexy."

"You wild thing," he said.

"Should we ditch Ari and work out all this sexual tension in your car?"

As much as he liked the idea, he had to pass. "Your sister doesn't trust me."

"That's not true! She likes you a lot."

"Sure," he said. "But she doesn't trust me around *you*."

Sasha took a bite of cherry pie and considered his words. "You've got it wrong," she said. "She doesn't trust *me* around you."

At that moment, Ariana came rushing back. "Oh God," she said. "That does look good. I'll have to try the cherry pie. We can run it off tomorrow."

"Who's we?" Sasha said, and handed her a spoon.

"You and me," Ariana replied. "Get ready. Tomorrow is a packed day, and we're starting off with a quick run. I've booked facials with the local esthetician at Pure—you know I had to find one. We have to stop by the calligrapher at some point, maybe after lunch. We'll finish the day with a girl's night in. Ex is coming home the following day, so we have to make the most of it."

The waiter poured their coffees. Nik took a spoon of apple pie to sweeten his bitter disappointment; he was certain he wouldn't see Sasha again for the next couple days.

"Have you tried the trails of North Cove Park?" he asked. "It overlooks a pink granite quarry. It's great for hiking."

"Sounds beautiful," Sasha said. "Do you hike there?"

"When I am in town. It's peaceful."

"Is it far?" Ariana asked.

"It's a quick drive. I'll send you the directions."

"How about you meet us there tomorrow?" Ariana proposed. "Seven thirty a.m. Are you up for it?"

Nik met Sasha's eyes and saw the silent plea there. "Why not? My first meeting isn't until ten."

"Will you join us for facials, too?" Sasha teased.

"I'll pass on that," he said. "Although it does sound good."

"It's settled," Ariana said. "Now that you're meeting us, I won't have any trouble dragging Sasha out of bed."

Twelve

Ari was the early riser. Sasha was the restless sleeper who had to hit the snooze button once or twice before dragging herself out of bed. Not this morning. She was up before her sister and knocking on her door. "Come on! Let's go!"

"You can come in, you know!" Ari hollered back.

Sasha found her sitting at the edge of her bed, fastening her running shoes. "I didn't pack hiking boots," she said.

"Since when do you hike?" Sasha asked.

"Ex and I go on regular hikes back in LA."

"Of course you do," Sasha said. "Let's get moving. I don't want Nik to wait too long."

"Of course not," Ari said with a wry smile. "How's it going between you two?"

"We're friends," she replied far too quickly. "What else can we be?"

"I know you like him, Sasha. But you're doing the right thing. Prioritize your well-being. Don't rush into anything."

Sasha avoided her sister's penetrating glare. "Uh-huh."

Ari hopped to her feet. "Let's go!"

On the ride to the park, Sasha debated whether she should just come clean with Ariana. She had no intention of prioritizing her well-being, of sacrificing passion for inner peace. She had no choice, really. It was as if she and Nik had bought two tickets on an insane roller-coaster ride the minute they boarded that plane in Atlanta. There was no getting off.

He wanted her. When was the last time anyone had said that to her so clearly? There were never any games with him. He was serious and straightforward in all things. She'd never met anyone so in command of himself. If only some of that could rub off on her.

Nik was waiting by his car at the North Cove parking lot. Wearing sunglasses, shorts and a white T-shirt that looked so soft. His short, barely there hair glistened from a shower. As always, his brown skin turned honey in the sun. Sasha wanted to bolt out of Ariana's Mercedes and run to him like a puppy let off her leash.

He greeted her with a knowing smile. "Sasha, good morning."

"Good morning to you," she said. "Ready to hike?"

"We can just walk, you know," he said. "The views are great."

"Thank God," Sasha said. "Tell it to her."

Ariana came around the hood of the car. "Tell me what?"

"Nik says—" Sasha reached out for Nik's hand and stopped herself just in time. The gesture felt so natural, refraining from it was forced.

"Says what?" Ari asked.

"Let's start slow," Nik replied on her behalf. "We can pick up the pace as we go."

"Sounds reasonable." Ari slipped on dark sunglasses for anonymity, no doubt. Only they made her look even more like a movie star. "Let's go."

Ten minutes into the run/hike/walk, Ariana's phone buzzed in her hand. She glanced at the screen. "Rylee!" she cried. "I have to get this."

She scurried off to the side to talk in private.

"Who's Rylee?" Nik asked.

"The wedding planner," Sasha replied. "The plan is top secret. It's all very hush-hush."

"Because of that wedding crasher dude sneaking around?" Nik asked.

"Yeah, but also because Ariana is taking this to the crazy place."

"Understood," Nik said. "You look beautiful."

Sasha acknowledged the compliment with a shrug. She hadn't worn her most shapely leggings for nothing.

They moved to the shade of an oak tree. A carving on the bark read: A-JACKS 4EVER <3. Sasha traced the letters with her finger. "Cute."

"According to Oliver, this place turns into lovers' lane by sundown," Nik said.

"Should we meet here at midnight?" Sasha said, only partly teasing.

"God, no," he said. "How about dinner? I'll make reservations somewhere nice."

"God, no." Sasha mimicked his tone. "I'm done running around Royal. Could we hang out at your place, order in?"

"How about tomorrow night?"

Tomorrow night. Two words never held so much promise. “It’s a date.”

Ariana came skipping back. “Guys! I just got off the phone with Ex.”

Sasha tore her gaze away from Nik, from that mouth she wanted to kiss, and those strong arms she needed to feel around her waist. “Uh… thought you were on the phone with Rylee.”

“Yes, and then I called Ex to update him on the plans,” Ari explained, as if it should have been obvious to anyone. “I told him we’ve been hanging out with Nik.”

Sasha wanted to correct her. *She* had been hanging out with Nik, and Ari had been chaperoning as if she were a heroine of some regency romance.

“He wants us all to have dinner at Sheen tomorrow night when he gets back,” Ariana said. “Nik, what do you say? Are you in?”

Sasha felt as if she might explode, particularly when Nik said he was up for it. But what else could they do but accept? Xavier was one of his top clients and her future brother-in-law.

Ari squealed. “It’s settled! Give me a minute to send Ex a quick text.”

She wandered off again. Sasha whirled around

to confront Nik, in jest. “How could you? We had plans!”

He raised an eyebrow like she knew he would. “Should I have told her I was planning to seduce you tomorrow night? Think that might have gone over better?”

Sasha stepped closer, hands on her hips. “When *do* you plan on seducing me then?”

Nik gave this some thought. “I’ll break you out of confinement tonight. Meet me by the service elevators.”

“Knowing Ari, she’s set up motion detectors.”

He slipped off his sunglasses and rubbed his eyes. “I’m fresh out of ideas. We’re screwed.”

Sasha burst into laughter. Nik laughed, too. Ariana returned to find them both laughing hysterically. “Hey! What’s so funny?”

“Never mind!” Sasha squeaked. She was breathless. “It’s late. Let’s hike!”

Later, at the esthetician’s office, Sasha received notification from the hotel where she was meant to stay for the remainder of her trip. She could check in tomorrow as early as noon. She shared the news with Ariana.

“You don’t have to leave us,” she said. “I made

that reservation for you weeks ago. Now that you're with me, I want you to keep you close."

"You and your fiancé deserve some alone time," Sasha said. "And I don't want to be anywhere around you when you get busy…so to speak."

"But Sasha—"

"But nothing, Ari!" She borrowed one of her sister's favorite phrases. "It's settled!"

"What if Ex spends a few extra days at his cousin's place?" Ariana proposed.

"Ari, stop," Sasha said wearily. "You don't have to babysit me."

They were sitting alone in the spa's chic waiting area. Sasha reached for her sister's hand and clasped it between her own. It was slowly dawning on her that Ariana's micromanaging was a symptom of a greater problem, as her therapist would say. "What are you worried about?" she asked.

"This can't be easy," Ari said. "My wedding is triggering all this stuff for you. I want you to know that I'm sensitive to that."

Tears sprung from Sasha's eyes. This was her fault for bringing up "the curse" on her first night. This was a special time for Ariana. She was marrying a wonderful man and deserved to enjoy this time.

"I'm so lucky to have you in my life," Sasha said. "You're my star, and I'd be lost without you."

"And you're my favorite person in the world," Ari said. "I'd do anything for you."

Sasha twisted in the leather armchair to face her. "There *is* something I need."

"Name it. Anything at all."

Sasha met Ari's wide brown eyes. "Anything?"

"Yes. I promise," Ari said. "Do you need money?"

"I need space."

Ariana made a face. "Oh."

"I've been living on my own a long time and enjoying it," Sasha explained. "I want to spread out, set up a mini studio, and work on a few projects while I'm here. That doesn't mean I won't be available for cake tastings and dress fittings. We'll see each other every day. I want to be a part of all of it. Your wedding day is my big special day, too."

"Alright," Ariana said. "I'll give you space."

The technician escorted them into the treatment rooms. As she lay on her back with thick cream slathered on her face, a tingle of excitement rushed through her. She couldn't wait to tell Nik that she was finally free!

Almost immediately, a shiver of fear chased away her excitement. Ariana wasn't unreasonable in urging her to slow down. After she broke off her engagement, things were bleak for a long while. In the months and years that followed, she'd lost a person she loved and the friendship forged through college. Their mutual friends sided with Terrence. Not only that, they took measures to protect him. They did not invite her to events when he was expected to attend; this meant birthday parties, brunches and weekend trips. Sasha found herself alone a lot. She left San Bernardino for San Francisco for a work opportunity, but really to escape the long shadow of her mistake.

Only, it wasn't a mistake. She could not have married Terrence.

When Ariana had called her with the news of her engagement, Sasha asked how she knew Xavier was the "one."

"It's not just *one* thing," she replied. "Let's start with the way he looks at me. People look at me all the time, but never like that. For such a confident, even cocky, person, he's kind of shy around me. It's endearing. He makes me feel protected and loved, like no one else can. So, we were at this crowded rooftop bar, right? Some guy was trying to take a photo of me. Ex wasn't having it. I told him to let it go. I didn't want to make a scene. He went and confronted the guy and had him delete the photo. I didn't have the heart to tell him that nearly everyone at that bar had posted photos of us and we were already trending on social media. And when we're alone together, we never run out of things to talk about. We have our silly jokes. His text messages make me smile. It's everything about him."

Ariana's words freed Sasha of any lingering doubts. Terrence was *not* the one for her. Her only regret was the way she'd gone about things. She should have never said yes to marrying him, should have never worn his ring. That serious lack of judgment troubled her. Her reasoning at the time was: Take a chance! Her motto now was: Take no chances. Which was proving to be just as harmful.

She liked Nik. She *really* liked him. She turned to sugar whenever he was around. The fires that he set in her soul just by looking at her never died down. She was more playful and flirtatious with him than she'd ever known herself to be. Nik wasn't Terrence. He knew her secrets and liked her anyway. He respected her work. He made her feel safe, like no one else could. To her mind, their attraction was worth exploring, even if it went nowhere, even if it meant risking all the progress she'd made.

Thirteen

Xavier returned earlier than expected. Ariana's cries of delight could drill a hole in concrete. Sasha was up and brewing her first cup of coffee when the sound of the key in the lock had her sister bolting to the front door. He lifted her off the ground and spun her around.

Only the most hardened cynic wouldn't be moved by their love.

"Hey Sasha!" Ari cried. "Look who's back!"

Sasha waved hello from the kitchen doorway. "Welcome home, Ex."

Her future brother-in-law beamed. "Welcome to you, Sasha! Ariana is so happy you're here. Did you two have fun?"

"We got into all sorts of trouble," Sasha said.

Xavier Noble flashed his trademark smile. It was similar to the one he flashed at late-night talk show hosts, but with a hint of shyness. "I want to hear all about it."

"Not before you take a shower," Ari said.

Ex made his eyebrows dance. "It's just a little sweat. Fishing is hard work."

"Go on," Ari said. "There are fresh towels in our bathroom. I'll make you coffee."

Ex drew her close and pressed his forehead to Ari's. "Thank you, honey."

Sasha swiveled on her heels and returned to the kitchen. When Ari joined her, she wore a silly little grin.

"Still want me to stay?" Sasha said. "Or could you two use some alone time?"

Ari rummaged through a jar of coffee pods for Xavier's favorite flavor. "You could go for a walk around the block for an hour or so."

"Do you have one of those Do Not Disturb door hangers?"

Ari pulled Ex's preferred mug that she'd brought from California out of the top cabinet. "I'll hang a tie."

Sasha grinned into her coffee cup and mumbled, “I’m outta here.”

Ari dropped everything onto the counter and rushed over to give her a hug. “I loved this time with you.”

Sasha let her sister hold and cradle and love her, and then she got out of her hair.

After his shower, Xavier took Sasha to the hotel. He waited as she checked in and wheeled her suitcases up to her room himself. “Just want to make sure you’re comfortable,” he said.

“I will be,” Sasha said. “This place is gorgeous. I’m starting to think all of Royal is a movie set.”

“It was a great place to grow up,” he said.

“Do you think you’ll ever return?” Sasha asked.

His answer warmed her heart. “Ariana is my home now. I want to be where she can thrive and that’s in LA.”

“Speaking of Ariana,” Sasha said. “She’s a little rattled by this wedding crasher stuff. The guy seems harmless enough, at least to me. She thinks he’s the Grim Reaper. Pro tip: whatever you do, don’t dismiss her concerns.”

“I hear you,” Ex said. “Thanks for looking out.”

They made it to her room on the tenth floor. Ex waved the key card and unlocked the door to a cozy suite complete with kitchenette. Some studio apartments in New York City weren't so well appointed. Ex brought her luggage into the bedroom. Sasha kicked off her sandals and made herself at home.

"So… Dinner tonight at Sheen?" Ex said on his way out.

"That's right," Sasha replied.

"And Nik is joining us?"

"Yep."

He'd texted earlier to confirm. She hadn't told him she was moving into the hotel. That was a surprise for later.

Ex lingered by the entryway. "You two are friends now?"

"It just happened. We flew in on the same plane."

"He's a great guy," he said. "I like him a lot."

Ex endorsing Nik's bid for her time was not on Sasha's bingo card, but there you had it. "I agree," she said. "He's awesome, and great in an emergency."

"Ari told me all about it."

"I bet she did." Sasha went to him and gently walked him out the door. "See you tonight!"

"We'll swing by and get you at seven."

"I'll be ready," she said. "And thanks again."

Sasha shut the door and leaned against it. She had lots to do. For starters, she had to unpack, then she had to pick a great dress to seduce a great guy.

Sheen was a glass house, all shimmer and shine. Ari pointed out that they could see the celebrity chef at work in the kitchen from the dining room. Sasha pointed out that she could see Nik already at the table, sipping water and looking like a snack in a dark suit. That last part she kept to herself. She brushed past the star couple as they meandered into the dining room, hopping from table to table, schmoozing and shaking hands. They'd catch up eventually, but her heart, her breath, every cell in her body were running ahead.

Nik locked eyes with her and rose to his feet. It took a glass house for her to see him clearly. Handsome, strong, steadfast. She might not walk down an aisle for this man, but she would walk on crushed glass.

His eyes raked over her body. His voice faltered as he said hello.

Sasha's dress was nothing more than wispy black silk held together by spaghetti straps. It was her secret weapon, packed at the last minute "just in case." She had no regrets.

He held out her chair and whispered, "I want to be good tonight. Why are you making it hard?"

"I'm sorry," she said. "The whole point of this dress was to make it hard."

Nik pushed out a laugh. They were giggling like naughty teens when Ari and Ex finally made their way to the table, hand in hand, sporting matching smiles.

"I feel like I'm meeting your parents," Nik said.

"Don't be ridiculous," Sasha said. "My parents are way more laid-back."

"Nikolai Williams," Ex bellowed. "Good seeing you again, man. Ari keeps raving about you."

Nik stood to shake Ex's hand. Ari went in for a full hug. Sasha's stomach did a little flip. She could picture a future in which nights like this were a regular occurrence, she and Nik meeting up with Ari and Ex for lunch, dinner and weekends away.

Ex started things off by asking typical dad

questions like "How's work?" Meanwhile Ari nodded her approval at Nik's answers. Sasha had the impression they were vetting him and wished they'd back off.

"I was really impressed by the way Nexus swooped in and bought my publisher's PR firm. It was aggressive. Good work."

Ex was this close to calling Nik "son."

"Oliver gets all the credit on that one," Nik said.

Ex brushed his words aside. "It was a team win."

"I wish it was always that easy," Nik said. "We're trying to swoop in on a company called Mad Dash, and we're not getting very far."

"I used Mad Dash while I was filming in Georgia," Ari said. "Their fees are manageable. I still have the app. Do they service Texas?"

"They don't. That's why we want to work with them. We see their potential for growth, but they won't meet with us."

"Their loss."

Between the appetizers and main course, Ari left the table to take a call from the executive producer of one of her projects. Between the main course and dessert, Nik had to step away to take a call from Oliver. He apologized and promised to turn off his phone for the rest of the night.

"Never mind," Ex said. "Do you think my future wife would ever turn off her phone?"

Ari smiled meekly. "Sorry, guys. I'm plugged in 24/7."

Before he left to take the call, Nik reached under the table for Sasha's hand and looped an index finger around her pinky in a sweetly possessive gesture. A million fireflies swirled around her heart.

As soon as he was out of earshot, Ariana said, "Do you know who's the CFO of Mad Dash?"

"How would I?" Unlike Nik, Sasha didn't read the *Royal Financial Times* for fun.

"Your old friend, Teresa Price!" Ari exclaimed.

"Really?" Sasha asked.

"Why do you think I downloaded the app in the first place?" Ari said. "Forbes posted about it on Instagram and I was curious. Turns out, I love it! Why don't you know about this? Don't you two keep in touch?"

Sasha crumbled inside. She and Teresa were not in touch. Teresa had gone to business school with her ex-fiancé and was "Team Terrence" all the way. Now her "old friend" was on the board of a company Nik was interested in. *Guess it's a small world after all.*

Over flourless chocolate cake, Ari asked Nik if he'd RSVP'd for the wedding.

"I did," he said. "Again, thanks for the invitation."

"Did you request a plus-one?" she asked.

"Ari!" Sasha cried.

"What?" Ari said. "We're just talking among friends."

"No," Nik said gracefully. "I don't have a plus-one."

"Well, you have one now!" With a flourish, Ari offered Sasha up as an all-purpose plus-one. "Sasha doesn't have a date, either. She loves to dance."

"Thanks for the intervention," Sasha said dryly. "We could've figured it out on our own."

"Sorry," Ari said. "Couldn't wait around for you to figure it out. Rylee has to finalize the seating chart."

"Rylee runs our lives," Ex said. "You'll get used to it."

Under the table, safe from view, Nik curled

his finger around hers once again. “I’d be more than honored to be Sasha’s date.”

“Good answer,” Ex said, and looked around for the waiter to request the check.

“Don’t mind that,” Nik said. “It’s taken care of.”

Ex and Ari thanked him in unison. Sasha took another sip of espresso to hide the fact that she was beaming with pride.

“Next time it’s on us,” Ari said.

“I’m looking forward to next time,” Nik said.

They rose from the table. This time there was less meandering. The four of them filed out of the dining room, chatting all the way, only to come to a full stop and crowd around the maître d’ station.

The thing with a glass house, however shimmery, it ultimately left you exposed.

Fourteen

Outside the door, paparazzi swarmed like angry bees. Sasha knew exactly why they were there. Before she could stop herself, she slipped her hand in Nik's. He squeezed it reassuringly.

"There's nothing we can do," the hostess said. "Someone must have tipped them off that you are here tonight."

Ari stepped behind Ex, her love and her shield.

"Don't worry," the hostess said. "We can see them, but they can't see us."

"Okay." Ari squared her shoulders, never one to display her weakness. "We'll just march through."

"No," Ex said firmly. "You're not up for this nonsense tonight, and I won't put you through it."

Nik stepped up. After conferring with the hostess who brought in the restaurant owner, Colin Reynolds, he came up with a plan.

"Sasha stays with me," he said. "Xavier, take Ariana out through the rear exit. Your car will be waiting. When you've made it out, send us a text. We'll wait until you're gone before we walk out."

This was Nik's superpower. He took charge and made sure everyone got home safe.

"You don't have to do that," Ari said, even though she was clearly relieved.

"It's already done," Nik said.

Ari turned to Sasha. "Do you mind?"

"Of course not!" Sasha pulled her into a hug and squeezed her tight. "Go! Run out back before they figure it out and camp out there, too."

Ex draped a protective arm over Ari's shoulders and led her away. They followed the hostess through the state-of-the-art kitchen. Sasha kept her eyes on them until they were out of sight. Then she stared at her phone until Ariana confirmed their safety with a thumbs-up emoji.

She looked up at Nik who was staring out at the mob of photographers. More than anyone, Sasha understood the value of capturing the right image at the right time. Getting photographed with the right people could boost a career. And still, she resented these men with cameras who made her sister's life difficult. She had a new understanding of the high price her sister paid to pursue her passions.

She touched Nik's arm. "They made it out. We can go."

Colin returned with a security guard. He confirmed that Ari and Ex had made it out safely. "Bill will escort you to your car."

"Good," Nik said. "Give us a minute." He slipped off his dinner jacket and draped it over Sasha's shoulders. She was instantly enveloped in his scent. "When they open the door, lower your head and stay close. I'll guide you out. Don't worry."

"I'm not worried," Sasha said. "They're not here for me."

"Even so," Nik said. "You're the maid of honor at one of the most talked-about weddings in the country. If they can get a piece of you, they will."

Sasha looked past his shoulders at the horde of photographers standing at the ready. She had never been at the receiving end of so much attention. She quivered with trepidation.

Bill opened the door. Nik drew her to him. Sasha nestled close and molded herself against his hard body. Head low, braids like a curtain around her face, Sasha fell in lockstep with Nik and let him guide her to safety, one more time.

Nik mostly kept his eyes on the road. Every now and then, he checked on her, his honey brown eyes flickered her way. "Are you okay?"

"I'm fine," Sasha said. "We've lived through worse."

"True." He reached for her hand. "Do I have to take you back straightaway?"

"I'm afraid so," Sasha replied. "Straightaway."

"Okay," he said flatly.

She let him stew in his disappointment before she revealed her secret. "I'll give you the address."

"I know it," he said, brows drawn in confusion.

"I'm not staying with my sister anymore," she said. "Please take me to Cascades Suites."

"Hold on. You moved out?"

"This morning," Sasha replied lightly. "Three's a crowd, you know what I mean?"

Nik withdrew his hand from hers. "And you waited until now to tell me?"

"No need to sound betrayed," Sasha teased. "It was a busy day. So, if you don't mind, take me straight to my hotel. I'd invite you up but the fridge is bare. I can't offer you a drink."

"I don't need a drink."

"Fine." Sasha slipped a key card in his pocket. "Cascade Suites is on Tenth and Lexington."

While Nik parked the car, Sasha went up to her suite. She tidied the mess she'd made in her bedroom while getting ready for dinner. Then she tackled the bathroom, freshening up before putting away her cosmetics. Twenty minutes passed and Nik still hadn't made it upstairs. What could be taking so long?

Finally, a knock on her door! She rushed to answer. "That took forever! Did you lose the key?"

Nik held up a bottle of wine and two glasses. Sasha knew exactly how he'd gone about getting it. "Who did you have to bribe to get that?"

"Never mind," he said. "Let me in."

She stepped aside. Before shutting the door behind them, she hung the Do Not Disturb hanger on the knob. Everything about tonight felt illicit and exciting, even though they were consenting adults and free to make their own mistakes.

This isn't a mistake.

Nik was in the kitchen, ripping the foil of the bottle.

"Stop!" she cried, and took the bottle from him. "We don't have time for an elaborate seduction."

"We don't?" Nik said. "Please don't tell me your sister is coming to check on you."

"No." She put the wine in the empty fridge and shut the door. "I don't need any more priming. We've had drinks, we've had pancakes for dinner, we've taken long strolls and picnicked in a garden, and tonight counts as a formal date, that's enough."

"You think this was for me?" Nik said. "This was for *you*. I'm ready."

To demonstrate how ready he was, he started on the buttons on his shirt.

"Let me."

Sasha brushed his hands away. She unfastened the little white buttons, starting at his collar, only to give up halfway and press her lips to the base of his neck. Nik let out a groan and gathered her into his arms. They kissed hungrily in her empty kitchen, tasting and feeding off each other. He slid his mouth down her neck and murmured, "You always smell so good."

Sasha pushed up against his lean, hard body. "And you always *feel* so good."

Nik gathered the silky fabric of her dress. "Take this off," he whispered hoarsely. "I want to see you."

Sasha stumbled away from him. "Good idea, actually. Everyone is responsible for removing their own clothes. We can do the sexy undressing another time."

Nik stripped off his shirt. "I appreciated your help, but you're too easily distracted."

She laughed and slipped her dress over her head. Could he blame her if she was excited?

Underneath her dress, she wore a simple bandeau bra and undies. The caramel color matched her skin perfectly. Nik fell back against the counter, and quietly took her in. "Oh, Sasha… How did I get so lucky?"

She let the dress fall to the floor and reached for his belt buckle. "If we weren't on that doomed flight, we might not have met. Can you imagine?"

"That would've been the real tragedy." He threaded his fingers through her braids as she struggled with the belt buckle with overly eager fingers. "Kiss me. I'll do the rest."

Sasha stretched onto her tiptoes and kissed him hotly. Nik gripped her behind and deepened their kiss. Why would she need wine if his kisses made her drunk?

"Take me to your bedroom," he whispered against her mouth. "Or I'll take you right here."

There was no time for location scouting. Her need for him was too great. "Take me right here."

He crushed her mouth with a kiss so demanding, her whole body started to pulse. He slipped a hand between her legs. "May I?" he said.

She caught his lower lip between her teeth. "Stop teasing me."

He pushed aside the damp panties and sunk his fingers into her wetness. Sasha tightened around him. Her head fell back as pleasure spread from her core up her spine.

He withdrew and placed both hands on her hips. He held her steady a moment then eased the underwear down and over her thighs. "It's not fair that you're still half-dressed," she said, as she readily stepped out of her underwear.

"It's not fair that I haven't seen my beauties yet. Let's set them free."

Nik walked her back against the refrigerator. He pushed her bra up and hungrily closed his mouth on her nipple. His teeth scraped against the sensitive tip. Sasha gasped and arched against the cold stainless steel. His fingers were inside her and his mouth was sucking her in. She twisted and whimpered, unsure she could take much more. She reached and felt for his erection and quickly withdrew her hand, stunned by what she found. "Oh, God, Nik..." She frantically pushed down at his waistband.

"Wait, wait, honey, wait..." Nik urged. From his pocket, he produced a wrapped condom. "Why do you think it took me so long to get here? I had to make a stop. I didn't expect this night to end this way."

Sasha thanked the heavens that one of them was still thinking straight. She plucked the foil packet and tore it open. "Take your clothes off," she ordered.

The clothes were off and the condom was on in under a minute. Sasha first cut off the overhead light, knowing the image of Nik's long, lean, taut body was forever stored in her imagination.

He grabbed hold of her waist and lifted her

onto the cold stone countertop. It didn't feel quite right. "Sorry!" she said. "I've changed my mind."

Nik stepped back. "You want to stop?"

"NO!" Shivering with want, she reached for him and yanked him back between her legs. "I changed my mind about the kitchen. It's not… giving what I thought it would."

He agreed. "We're too sober for this."

"I guess we'll have to do it the old-fashioned way." Sasha sighed, resigned. "To the bedroom!"

"Let's go!"

In one smooth move, Nik picked her up off the counter and hauled her onto one shoulder. Sasha squealed. "You caveman! Put me down!"

"Point the way."

"It's the door to the left!" she cried. "My left!"

The door was ajar. Her caveman kicked it wide open and flopped her onto the bed. Sasha shook with laughter. Nik stood at the foot of the bed, grinning, proud of his prowess. His erection, though, was proudest of all.

She extended her arms. "Come to me."

Nik crawled onto the bed. All laughter subsided when he brushed her braids away from her face and coaxed her to look at him. "This current between us," he said. "I've felt it since the day we met. Say you felt it, too."

Sasha nodded. Her throat was too tight to speak.

Nik brushed his lips to hers. "Say it."

"You know I did," she said, her voice thin.

He dragged his nose down her neck. "Yes, but I want to hear it."

"I felt it the first time you looked at me," Sasha said.

"On the plane?" he murmured against her skin.

She shook her head, her breath shallow. "Not on the plane."

"When?"

"When I found you at the airport coffee shop."

He kissed her. "You found me."

"Yes." Sasha wrapped her legs around his waist. "Now come find me."

He held her still and eased inside her. She couldn't help but tighten around him. "Sasha…" he whispered.

She buried her face in his chest. "Oh my God… please…"

That was the moment Nik lost his fantastic self-control. He entered her fully and they started moving, effortlessly finding a rhythm all their own. She gripped his arms and when that wasn't enough she bit his shoulder. Nik teased and called her his wild one. Pleasure rolled through her, she lost the trail of his voice. She could only feel him inside her, all around her.

Come find me.

She wrapped her legs tighter around his waist. He burrowed deeper and deeper still, nudging her up to the edge of a cliff. Sasha would have happily toppled into an abyss of pleasure, but Nik wouldn't let her. He withdrew and fell onto his back and motioned for her to straddle him.

"Okay, fine!" she said begrudgingly. "I'm in charge."

He laughed softly into the darkness. "No, honey, you're not. I want to watch you, that's all."

"Oh, is that all?" Sasha's laugh was wild and wicked. She was going to ride this man to the ground.

As it turned out, that was wishful thinking on her part. She couldn't stand to be apart from him for too long. She bent low for a quick kiss. His fingers tangled in her braids and, despite his earlier claim, he kept her close. Heat roped them together, ever tightening, until she could barely breathe, until the rope snapped and sent her into free fall.

Fifteen

Out of breath, his body still crackling with desire for her, Nik stared up at the ceiling. "Sasha… why did we wait for so long to do this?"

"We literally waited three days," she replied. "That's not very long by most standards."

"Whose standards are we playing by?" he asked.

"Society?"

"I hate society," he grumbled.

"Me, too. They ruin everything." Sasha curled up to him and pressed the palm of her hand to his sternum. "Did I tell you that I love your body?"

He ran a hand down the curve of her side. "Did I tell you that I'm obsessed with yours?"

She laughed and said, "You're right. We should've done this sooner. We should've joined the Mile High Club as the plane came crashing down."

Nik tried to picture it. "That's a story for our grandchildren."

Her face clouded and he regretted the joke almost immediately.

"I didn't mean it," he said. "It was just a joke."

"I know that!" she said, brightening all too suddenly.

He cupped her face to reassure her, even as an image sharpened in his mind: children, grandchildren, a lifelong road trip of adventures with this woman. It scared him to death. Sasha would never agree to any of that.

Here he was, back where he'd started. He loved the wild ones, and the wild ones had to run free.

Nik had dismissed his cousin's concerns the night they'd discussed his personal life over margaritas. He told her she was way off course.

"It's because of your parents," Krystal said.

"Not everything is because of our parents," he said.

"Maybe, but in this case we can draw a straight line to your dad leaving and your mother—"

"Hold on," he said, interrupting her. "If I follow your logic, my dad was the wild card of my family. He took off and never looked back. Why would I chase after that? My mother was steadfast, steady. I admire her so much. To this day, she's my hero."

"Pardon my saying this, but your mom, who happens to be my beloved godmother and aunt, was tired, overworked, a little cranky and always complaining about money—"

"Come on! How can you blame her for that?"

"I don't blame her," Krystal said. "Don't put words in my mouth."

"Then what?"

"Of course, you admire her strength and appreciate her sacrifices," Krystal went on. "You're not a monster. But your dad got to run free. He got to be a supernova, a rock star. That's the quality that you're chasing after."

Nik tried to make sense of her words. Maybe he'd had too much to drink, but he found it too abstract a concept for him to grasp.

"Sorry," he said. "I don't see it."

"You may not be ready to admit it now," Krystal said. "You're a smart guy. One day, you'll figure it out."

He'd figured it out, all right. Here and now, in Sasha's bed.

He ran a hand over his face. Sasha pulled it away. "What's wrong?"

"Nothing's wrong," he said.

"Why do you look like that?" she asked.

"No reason."

"Listen, I can take a joke."

"I know, honey," he said. "It's not that. I should get going now."

She drummed his chest with her fingertips. "Tomorrow is Saturday. Do you have to work?"

"No, actually. I don't."

"Why leave, then? We have so much lost time to make up for."

She stared up at him with wide, pleading eyes. Nik didn't want to leave her. In all honesty, he didn't think he could. But he didn't want to stay here and dream of their grandchildren, either. It was all moving so fast. It had only been three days…

"Do you want me to stay?" he asked, at a loss.

"I'm practically begging you," Sasha said. "Come on…*please*."

"Okay, I'll stay," he said. "We'll have to order

groceries, though. Your refrigerator has exactly one bottle of wine."

"There's also some icicles in the freezer," she said. "A welcome gift from the hotel."

He propped himself up on an elbow. "This just got real," he said. "Let's compile a grocery list."

Sasha got up and stretched languidly on her way to the bathroom. "Order enough for two days. I don't think I'm going to let you out."

Nik looked up from his phone. "Most women just ask me to spend the night."

"I'm not most women, Nik!" she said, balking.

Standing at the bathroom doorway, naked, veiled only with light, her braids long and loose on her back, Sasha was surreal. Nik had to agree. She was unlike any woman he had ever met in his life.

"Those women have their lives together," she said. "They're way more secure than I am. I'm needy. Right now I need more of your time. Spend the weekend with me."

At this point, rabid dogs couldn't chase him away. She didn't need to know that. "I'm staying," he said. "And I'm ordering ice cream."

"Do what you must!" She moved to shut the bathroom door and stopped. "This weekend is just for us. We can say and do whatever we like. I don't want to see that worried look on your face ever again!"

Nik stared at the closed door. Sasha locking him up in her bedroom for a weekend was sexy as fuck, and here he was analyzing his past and dreaming about grandchildren. He had to get his head back in the game.

Sixteen

There were some things they couldn't order in, like a change of underwear. For that reason alone, Sasha agreed for Nik to return to his place in the morning for the limited purpose of packing a bag. It wasn't like her to be so straightforward and demanding, so *clingy*, but the moment had called for it. She wanted him. Her time at Ariana's place should have been a cooling-off period. Instead, it fueled her desire. He wanted her, too. There was no doubt in her mind he felt the same way. That stupid joke about grandchildren had sent her into a tailspin and he must have misread her reaction.

Sasha knew he was joking. Nik was a reasonable person. He wasn't thinking about grandkids or a future together after their first roll in the sack, but she was. Just like at the restaurant, she caught a glimpse of it, a future for her and Nik that might include a brood of bossy and opinionated children. Far from freaking her out, it had pleased her to her core. *That* was scary.

Nik kissed her goodbye. "I won't be long."

She wrapped her arms around his neck. "Are you sure you're not going to run for your life?"

"No," he said in his serious voice. "I'm running right back to you so we can lock this door and keep it locked for the next forty-eight hours."

"I like the sound of that."

"Not as much as me. I'll be back."

He kissed her again and was gone. Sasha could not sit still. She wanted to do cartwheels. She couldn't believe it. She and Nik had the weekend to themselves. They deserved this, if only for surviving the trip to Royal. She was going to make it wonderful for him. They would talk, cook, make love, watch television shows and just be together. It was going to be glorious.

A knock on her door knocked her back to her senses. Nik?

She opened the door. “Did you forget something?”

“What do you mean? Did you leave something behind at the apartment?”

It was Ari, dressed in black linen and sporting her black sunglasses. Sasha blinked, confused. Were they supposed to meet today?

“I left my hairbrush,” Sasha said absently.

“Your hair is in braids.”

She ran her hair through her tangled braids. “Right.”

“Are you busy?” Ari asked.

“Yes.”

“Come with me. It won’t take long.”

“Where are we going? And why are you acting so weird?”

“Never mind,” Ari said. “I’ll have you back in no time. I promise.”

Damn. There was no way out of this! “Okay. Give me a second. I have to put on my sneakers and grab my phone and…”

“Just hurry. I’ll use your bathroom.”

“No!”

Ari paused. “Why no?”

There was an open box of condoms on the bathroom vanity. That was why.

"I'll take you to the one off the lobby," Sasha said. "It's pink marble and perfect. So lovely! You'll love it."

"It doesn't matter," Ari said. "We don't have time. Let's just go."

Ariana drove them to the center of town, to the chic shopping plaza they'd visited on their last outing. She parked across the street from the florist's boutique.

"Why are we here?" Sasha asked, arms folded across her chest. "Is there some flower emergency? A shortage of bluebonnets in the great state of Texas?"

Ariana ripped off her seat belt and tilted her seatback. "Get low," she said. "We're incognito."

"Are we, though?"

They were driving around in a black Mercedes that she was pretty sure anyone could identify as Xavier's. They weren't fooling anyone.

"What's the point of all this, Ariana?" Sasha demanded. "Aren't we going in?"

"We're on a stakeout."

"Are you kidding me?"

"I'm not," Ari said bluntly. "*He*'s in there."

"*Who*'s in there?"

"The wedding crasher."

"Jesus Christ!" Sasha reached for the door handle and pushed the door open. "I'm going to talk to him."

Ari grabbed her by the arm and yanked her back in. "Stay here! I'm not even sure he's in there. I got a tip and wanted to see for myself."

Unbelievable!

"So what if he's in there?" Sasha said. "What can you do? He has every right to be in a public place. Who knows? He might be buying flowers for his girlfriend."

"He's not buying flowers for anyone. I can tell you that!" Ari snapped. "He's trying to get our florist, Corynna, to spill to spill. This is how he operates. He asks innocent questions of the cashier or some unsuspecting employee. They share a silly anecdote and from those bits and pieces he constructs his story."

"Such a man is on the loose and the FBI hasn't recruited him?" Sasha pondered. "This country has lost its edge."

"Joke around all you want," Ari said. "*My* wedding is big business for a guy like him."

"Here's my issue," Sasha said. "You said this wasn't going to take long. In my limited experience, watching movies and TV shows, a stakeout can last for hours. I didn't sign up for that."

"Doubt it," Ari said. "How long can anyone stay in a flower shop?"

"Which brings me to my next issue. What if he's already gone?"

Ari didn't have a quick answer to that.

"What if I go inside just to take a quick look?" she proposed. "I won't approach him. I'll use my superpowers to figure out exactly what he's up to."

"Your superpowers," Ari said, pausing to add air quotes, "won't work in this case. The shop has one of those old-timey bells above the door. As soon as you walk in he'll be alerted of your presence."

Sasha threw her hands up. "Sorry, Ari, I don't see the point of this. And next time we go on a stakeout, buy me an ice coffee first."

"I don't see the point, either," Ari admitted. She slipped off her sunglasses and covered her eyes with her hands. "Rylee said that he was poking around the flower shop and I rushed out in a rage."

"Ex didn't try to talk you out of it?" Sasha seriously questioned her future brother-in-law's judgment. She'd asked him not to dismiss Ari's feelings. That didn't mean he should let her act on those feelings. There was a line that logic didn't cross.

Ari sighed. "Ex doesn't know. He was working when I left the apartment."

"Ah." That made sense.

Ari's shoulders dropped in defeat. "I just want this wedding to be perfect, you know?"

"It can't be perfect," Sasha said. "You'll never have the picture-perfect wedding of your little girl dreams. How could you? Our aunts and uncles will be there. Our tribe of cousins, too. We're not country-club type people. It's gonna get wild. A wedding crasher is the least of your problems."

"Oh, God!" Ari moaned. "You're so right. When the DJ switches to House music it's going to get loud."

"Exactly!"

"Hey!" Ari exclaimed. "Why can't you show yourself that same grace?"

"Excuse me? I don't know what you mean."

"Your life isn't perfect. You had some setbacks. Maybe now it's time to lay it all to rest and move on with someone new, don't you think?" Ari explained. "Have you given any thought to what I said about Nik?"

"Uh… You said to stay away from him."

Ari bristled. "That's what I said, but that's not what I meant."

"What did you mean, then?"

"To wait until you were sure," Ari said. "I thought I made that point clear."

"Oh."

Ari touched her arm. "Nik is into you. That's obvious to everyone. All I asked was for you to take it slow, not to dismiss it as a fling."

This was the time to come clean to her sister and tell her that she and Nik were way past taking it slow. They'd burned through every red light. That wasn't what Ariana wanted to hear. Even though it felt rare and special and real, it pretty much had all the trappings of a fling. They hadn't discussed the future, not even the immediate future beyond this weekend. Ariana would have questions and she had no answers. Her mind was as bare as her refrigerator. So, she kept quiet.

"I guess we should head back now," Ari said. "This was stupid."

"Yeah…" Sasha agreed.

"I won't do it again."

"Good."

"What will I tell Ex? He'll think I lost my mind."

"Don't tell him," Sasha said. "This can be our little secret."

"Yeah, right," Ari said. "In five years you'll tell the whole family the story at Christmas."

Sasha winked. "More like next year. It's a great story."

Nik was home, unpacking groceries, when Sasha got back. "Hey! Where were you?" he said. "I sent you a text."

The sight of him in the tiny kitchen stirred up memories of the night before and all the things they'd been up to since.

"Sasha? Are you okay?"

"I'm not okay! I was kidnapped by my sister!"

"What?"

"She got word that the wedding crasher guy was at the flower shop, and she wanted to stake it out."

"Are you kidding?"

"I wish I were."

Nik put a quart of ice cream in the freezer.

"Has he done anything all that bad? He hasn't revealed anything specific. From what you've shown me, he's dealing in speculation."

"Tell that to Ari," Sasha quipped. "She's convinced he has the power to ruin her wedding."

"She's stressed."

"And she's stressing me out." Sasha slipped off her sneakers and padded barefoot into the sitting room.

"Why don't you pull up those videos," Nik suggested. "Let's see how bad it can get."

"Really?"

Why did this simple request make her so unreasonably happy? She'd been secretly binge-watching Trick MacArthur's YouTube channel, and feeling intense shame about it. It was by definition a guilty pleasure. Ariana would kill her if she found out. Here, Nik presented the opportunity to do so in a guilt-free way. *Let's see how bad it can get.* This was research. Really, they were doing Ariana a favor, looking out for her.

For the next half hour, they sat on the couch, snacking on chips, watching the videos on the wall-mounted TV, pausing now and then to argue a point or break out in laughter. The Carlisle wedding had them rolling with laughter.

Nik hit Pause. “I can’t believe she picked that ugly dress. I don’t care who designed it or how much it costs.”

Sasha wiped tears from her eyes with the back of her hands. “Don’t say that! Brides are like babies. They’re all beautiful.”

“She’s lovely. That dress is *not*,” Nik said. “Trick was right.”

“Trick is always right. Ariana should be taking notes.”

Nik stretched out and propped his head on a throw pillow. “That’s a lot to go through to get married.”

Sasha folded her legs underneath her. “How would you like to get married?”

“Something small with family and only the closest of friends,” he said without hesitation.

“Me, too,” Sasha said. “When you’re rich and famous, a wedding becomes an event. The photos are sold and the public gets to pick apart your choices down to the cake flavor. I’m glad I’m not famous. Although, I wouldn’t mind being rich.”

“Do you like where you are, career-wise?” he asked.

“It’s going well, so far. Obviously, photographers don't make too much money until they win a Pulitzer."

He tilted his head, looked at her through narrowed eyes. "Is that something you aspire to?"

She nodded, unable to say the words. It made sense that Ariana would win an Oscar someday, either as an actor or director. Those same shiny statues were always out of her reach. "I'd like to do something worthwhile with my talent and my tools."

"The work you did for *New Day* magazine was exceptional."

"Thank you."

"I mean it," he said. "It must have been taxing, too."

"It was."

The magazine had sent her to Kansas after a tornado had ravaged a small town. It was heartbreaking work, but necessary. Video was great; however, nothing captured the emotional weight of a moment better than photography.

"I think you're a genius and an artist," he said. "Not only that, I think you'll win that Pulitzer."

"How about you?" she asked. "What does the future look like for you?"

"I'm sort of drifting," he replied. "I sold my Miami Beach condo."

Sasha sat up straighter. "That's right. You mentioned it."

"I didn't care for the place. So when I was offered three times the amount I'd paid for it, I let it go."

"Will you stay in Royal?" she asked.

"I'm not needed in Royal," he said. "Oliver has it covered. It's not where the action is, at least in my mind."

Sasha wondered where that might be. New York, maybe?

Nik set the bag of chips he'd been munching on to the side and wiped his hands on a napkin. "Should you ever consider getting married, how would you go about it?"

"I…um…" Sasha looked down at her hands. "I'd…um…"

"If it makes you uncomfortable, we don't have to talk about it."

She wanted to talk about it. Her past mistakes shouldn't keep her from dreaming of a future. Sasha believed in the power of visualization. It made her good at her job. She had to picture a future in which she was happy and fulfilled or else it would never happen.

"I'd put on a minidress, grab a bouquet of tulips and dash off to San Francisco City Hall on a Friday afternoon. Afterwards I'd host a big family dinner at my airy loft overlooking the Golden Gate Bridge."

Nik went silent for a while. Sasha's heart felt exposed in her chest. She didn't breathe until he extended his arms. "Come to me."

Seventeen

If she believed in curses, then Nik had no reason to doubt that she had cast a spell on him. When she melted in his arms and kissed him slowly, pulled away and tugged off his clothes, traced every line of his body with her fingertips and tongue and finally gave him what he thought he'd wanted the night before but couldn't handle, straddling him, magnificent, head tossed back, braids cascading the length of her spine, until he gripped her by the waist and got her where she wanted to go, then collapsed into his arms, her heart pounded into his chest—when she'd done all that, Nik knew he was under a spell. There was no talisman, no charm, no mantra he could repeat three times to free him from it. Everything in him was now linked to Sasha.

The weekend went by all too fast. One moment, he was holding Sasha while she slept, loving her in the shower, spoon-feeding her ice cream in the kitchen, the next he was back at work.

On Monday morning, bright and early, Nik was discussing the chances of the local tennis champion at Wimbledon with Mavis, the office building's security guard. That's where Oliver found him, coffee cup in hand, while Mavis mimed the killer backhand that would secure the tennis pro's victory.

"I don't know," Nik said. "I still like Naomi Osaka's chances."

"This is *our* chance to bring the trophy home to Texas!"

Oliver grabbed his elbow and dragged him off to the elevators. "I support Texas!" he called out to Mavis. Once in the car, he hit the button to the sixteenth floor and said, "Nah. It's Naomi for the win."

"Right?" Nik said. "No doubt about it."

Oliver ran a hand through his hair. "How was the weekend? I got some stuff done, but not much. You?"

Nik took a sip of black coffee. He was going to need several cups to make it through the day. "I fell in love with Sasha Ramos this weekend."

Oliver dropped his laptop case. "What did you just say?"

"I didn't get anything done," Nik said. "I'm going to lock myself in my office and double down on—"

"Hold on! Back up! I don't care about work."

Nik blinked at him. "What?"

"You said you fell in love with Sasha Ramos this weekend."

"Oh, shit…"

"Oh, yeah!" Oliver laughed and picked up his laptop case off the elevator floor. "You were going to speed past that?"

Nik let out a groan. "I didn't mean to say that."

"Nice! We're keeping secrets now?"

The elevator opened to their floor. Oliver gripped Nik's arm and steered him into his office. Although the floor was empty at this hour, he shut the door behind them for added privacy. Nik fell onto one of the two armchairs facing the desk.

Oliver paced the floor. "So, like, what? You

stared across a crowded room and fell in love with Ariana Ramos's little sister?"

Nik chafed at his description of Sasha. People weren't willing to let her out of Ariana's shadow. "Let's not call her 'little.' She's a woman."

"I'm sure you know all about that," Oliver quipped.

Yeah, he did, but that was neither here nor there. "I'm just saying there's more to her than that."

"I'm concerned how our *client*, worldwide bestselling author Xavier Noble, will take it, that's all."

"I wouldn't worry," Nik said. "We all had dinner Friday night."

Oliver threw his hands up. "Well, in that case!"

"I know what it looks like," Nik said.

"I don't think you do," Oliver said. "Your head is in the clouds."

Nik didn't deny it. He was a fool in love. "Sasha is amazing."

"Uh-huh," Oliver said. "So long as you keep her happy. We can't piss off one of our most famous clients. If she tells her sister and her sister tells her husband… See where I'm headed?

It can get messy. Now, I'm not judging you. I'm no stranger to mess."

Nik lifted the cap off his coffee cup and studied the contents. "It's not like that. Sasha is leaving after the wedding, and that's the end of it."

"Oh." Oliver sat at the corner of his desk. "How do you feel about that?"

He shrugged. "I'll deal with it."

He had no choice but to deal with it. He knew what he'd signed up for. No one had told him to fall in love with a woman who ran from love. That was on him. He would have to climb out of that wholly all on his own. It wasn't going to be easy, and it might take a lifetime. Even so, he didn't care. It was worth it to feel this way.

"When did all this happen?" Oliver asked. "Just the other night we ran into you and you claimed *not* to be on a date. I took your word for it."

"We weren't on a date," Nik said. "Obviously, things steamrolled from there."

Oliver let out a low laugh. "I bet!"

"People write poetry about what I lived through this weekend," Nik said.

"Stop! Spare me!" Oliver cried. "I'm getting goose bumps."

Nik rose to his feet. "Now you know everything. I got to catch up on work."

"Hold on. Not so fast," Oliver said. "Isn't she from the Bay Area?"

Nik shifted his weight from one foot to the other. He had a feeling where Oliver was headed, and he didn't like it. "Uh-huh."

"So, it's not as open-and-shut as you're making it sound," Oliver said. "You're relocating our office from LA to San Francisco by the end of the year."

"About that," Nik said. "I haven't told her, so please don't mention it."

"Uh...why? It's a solution to your problem."

Nik sat back down again. "The window passed. I should've mentioned it when we first met. Now it'll sound like I'm following her to her city. It'll be weird."

For someone as commitment averse as Sasha, it would likely creep her out.

"It'll be weird when you show up at her local coffee shop, one morning out of the blue, without her ever knowing that you were in town."

"San Francisco is a big city. We may never run into each other."

"Don't kid yourself. That's not how it works,"

Oliver said. "You'll run into her just as soon as you step out of the airport. You're going to have to tell her. The window isn't closed. I get that it may be a lot to spring on someone, but it may not be as bad as we're making it out to be. Just because you're moving to her city, doesn't mean you're moving into her apartment. San Francisco is big enough for both of you."

Nik took another sip of coffee only to find that the cup was empty.

Oliver was looking at him quizzically. "Oh, shit…" he said. "You don't think she feels the same about you. You're out there drowning in love. Meanwhile, she's safe on the shore."

Every muscle in Nik's body tensed. "It's not like that."

"Okay, buddy," Oliver said. "Tell me how it is."

"I don't want to scare her."

"She doesn't look like the type of person who scares easily," Oliver said. "Then again, I don't know her as well as you do."

Nik slumped in his chair. How did it get so complicated? The move to Silicon Valley was months in the planning. He wanted to be where tech innovation brewed, get on the ground floor of some of the most innovative start-ups. His work was at the core of his life. It thrilled and motivated him. He wanted to share his plans with her without her worrying that he was trying to crowd her.

"Obviously, honesty is the best policy," Oliver said. "You can bend the truth a little. Delay the move by a couple months. There's no rush. That way, if you run into her at her coffee shop, it won't be awkward. It'll be water under the bridge."

Oliver had a point. If he delayed the move, he wouldn't have to tell her anything. A year would have passed. They would be over each other, and he wouldn't owe her an explanation. The idea alone made him sick. A part of him couldn't believe he was second-guessing the plan to accommodate Sasha, yet he was. When you loved someone, you put her needs first. Sasha had been through too much. For all her toughness, she was more fragile than most. Oliver didn't know this, and he wouldn't understand.

He got up and went to the door. "I should get busy. Thanks for giving me 'the talk.' I'll think about what you said."

"Anytime!" Oliver said, grinning. "Hey, Nik?"

"Yeah."

"She's smart. She'll figure out that she's scored big with you."

* * *

By midday, Nik could no longer focus on anything. His talk with Oliver had unearthed too much. He shot a text to Krystal. Free to talk?

She promptly responded with a video call. Her grinning face filled the screen. She raised a glass of what looked like an Aperol Spritz. "*Buona sera*, cousin!" she said. "I'm enjoying an *aperitivo! Cin cin!*"

Nik pinched the bridge of his nose. "Is this how it's going to be all summer long?"

"Assolutamente!"

"My God…" Nik groaned.

Krystal excused herself from a group and ventured out to a terrace overlooking a quintessential Roman street, cobblestones and all. She had sent him her itinerary. After a few nights in Rome, she would settle in Milan to study classical drawing techniques.

"How do you like it so far?" Nik asked.

"What? Are you kidding me?" Krystal cried. "I'm living a dream!"

Nik was happy for her. Ever the dutiful daughter, she'd done everything to make her parents proud. She'd gone to college, instead of art school, and pursued a traditional career. It wasn't until her father had passed away that she gave herself permission to pursue the desires of her heart.

"You look radiant, and I'm proud of you."

"Aw!" she cooed. "Thanks, baby cousin! You look a little worn out. What's up?"

"Thought I'd call to tell you that you were right, and I'm an idiot."

"I already knew that," Krystal said. "What else you got?"

I love someone who loves to run. That was as far as the words would go. He didn't want Oliver's hot takes or Krystal's clinical advice. He wanted to talk to Sasha. Whatever her reaction, he would take it.

"That's it," he said. "That's all I got."

"Hey, listen," Krystal said. "I might've been a little harsh on you the last we talked. Who am I to tell you who to love or how to live your life? Of all of us, you've got your act together. Look at me in Italy spending a fortune on art classes, picking up a skill I'll never use in a professional capacity. If I think about it too much, I'll burst into tears."

"Krystal, if you want to pursue art in one way or another, no one can stop you," he said. "Even if the family tried to give you grief, I'd call each one of them up and set them straight."

She dabbed at a tear swelling in the outer corner of her eye. "You'd do that?"

"Damn right I would."

"Thank you," she said. "I needed to hear that today."

He'd called to talk out his issues. Of the two of them, she was the one who was in need of counseling and support. He was here for it. "Is everything alright?"

Krystal took a breath. "I don't think I can go on counseling athletes, encouraging them to pursue their dreams while I ignore my own."

"That makes total sense," he said.

"I don't think I am who I was meant to be," she said. "I ended up with a life that doesn't feel like mine."

Nik ached for her. Krystal was more than a cousin. She was the sibling he'd never had. If she wanted to live her life in Europe, studying art history and drawing ancient statues, then she deserved to try and fail, try again and succeed.

Similarly, if he wanted to chase a wild love, he shouldn't let anything get in his way. His father might have planted the seed in him, but he was his own man now. Nik would take his chances with Sasha. He'd rather chase a shooting star than wait, complacent, for one to fall on his lap.

"I have to join the others now."

"Go on," he said. "We'll talk soon."

"Ciao, bello!"

"Oh, shut up!"

"And good luck with the girl, whoever she is this time around! Go get her!"

Eighteen

Sasha spent Monday afternoon with Ariana. Her sister was more relaxed this time around and Sasha tried her best not to jinx it. She kept the conversation light and bubbly. At Natalie Valentine's Bridal Shop, she tried on her bridesmaid's gown for the first time, twirled in it, posed for photos, toasted with champagne and did not fidget during the fitting. Afterward, they stopped by the florist, approved a last-minute change to the centerpieces, checked out the bluebonnets, and the name "Trick" did not come up once.

"Thanks for hanging out with me today," Ari said.

"I meant what I said. I'm here for all of it," Sasha replied. "What's on the list for tomorrow?"

Ariana flashed a smile. "Tomorrow is a fun day. We meet with the mixologist and sample the signature cocktail. Ex is coming along for that one."

"Sounds like a good time."

They were on the sidewalk outside the shop, in plain sight of everyone, like normal people. Sasha was getting anxious.

"I know what you're thinking," Ari said.

"What's that?"

"You're wondering why I'm not ranting and raging about the wedding crasher."

"I was, actually."

Ari squared her shoulders. "I had a good cry last night and got it out of my system."

"Good for you. Maybe we should have this conversation in the car."

"It's okay, Sasha. I'm not running from paparazzi anymore."

"Why the hell not?"

That didn't seem wise. Sasha looked around just in case a photographer was lurking behind the esthetically pleasing recycle bin.

"Because I'm taking your advice."

That didn't seem wise, either. "Which advice?"

"I'm enjoying this time with its ups and downs," Ari said. "I'm enjoying my crazy circus of a wedding. With any luck, it's the only one I'll ever have."

"That's the spirit!"

"I don't know what I was thinking, dragging you into a stakeout on Saturday. I apologize."

"Don't get me wrong," Sasha said. "I'm all for a stakeout with proper notice. Had you told me what we were up to, I would've grabbed my camera, the one with the super lens. What's the point of a stakeout without incriminating photos?"

"You got a point there." Ari smiled. "Anyway, I wanted you to see for yourself that I'm calmer now. I don't want to worry you."

"Hey! That's my line!" Sasha cried. "I'm the lost soul. You're the bright shiny star. We picked those roles at birth. There's no going back."

"Nonsense!" Ari scoffed. "You're the most beautiful soul I know."

"I have my moments."

Ari checked her watch, a gold Cartier. "I'm meeting Ex for dinner. Want to join us?"

"Not tonight," Sasha said. Although she had no definite plans, she knew whom, if given a choice, she would rather have dinner with. "You two have fun. I'd like to wander around, do some window shopping."

Ariana left and Sasha wandered straight into an ice cream shop and bought a gourmet vanilla Popsicle dipped in Belgian chocolate and smothered in nuts. This could be dinner, she thought. She could catch up on reading or watch a movie…or…she could call Nik.

He'd left early this morning with a kiss goodbye. The question hung in the air long after he was gone: When will I see you again?

Sasha was reluctant to ask because she'd taken so much of his time already. Now she felt a little foolish for not asking. They had so little time to spend together, she didn't want to waste any of it by playing it safe.

She decided to send a feeler in the form of a selfie. She snapped a photo of herself biting into the ice cream bar.

His answer: Cute. Is that from earlier today?

Her response: No. That's from right now. I'm at the shops in Midtown.

Him: I know exactly where you are. Give me 5 minutes.

Sasha would've squealed in delight if she

weren't in public. This was what she loved about Nik. He was spontaneous, up for whatever and… coming around the corner, a wide grin on his face.

Sasha ran toward him. They crashed into each other.

Nik circled an arm around her waist. "I need a bite of that!"

Sasha laughed. "Of what, exactly?"

"Give me this."

He took a greedy bite of her Popsicle. Sasha kissed his cheek while he chewed. "Admit it. You came all this way just for the ice cream."

"Don't tease me with ice cream," he said. "I'll come running."

"Where did you come running from?" she asked.

"My office isn't far, neither is my rental apartment."

"Is that a fact?"

"It is," he said. "I'd invite you up, but I'm all out of champagne and caviar."

"Don't need it," Sasha said. "I had champagne at the bridal shop. I'm good."

"In that case, it's my turn to lock you up."

She slid her arms around his neck. "Please do."

He took another bite of ice cream. Sasha laughed; her eyes squeezed shut. When she opened her eyes again, the first thing she saw was a young man with wavy brown hair duck into the corner store.

"That bastard!" she swore under her breath.

Nik stepped away. "Who, me?"

"No, sweetie." She pressed a hand to his cheek to reassure him. "Not you. *Never* you."

"Who then?" He glanced over his shoulder, scanned around for the bastard.

"Trick! I saw him go into that shop."

"Which one?"

She pointed to the shop with the Popsicle. "That one."

"Christ," he mumbled.

"He's stalking Ariana," Sasha said. "She was here a moment ago. Someone must have tipped him off and now he's poking around."

"Want me to check it out?" he offered.

"No, I'll go," Sasha said. "This job calls for my superpowers. If he's poking around and asking questions, I'll figure out what he's after. That way, Ariana can get one step ahead of him."

"Bad idea," Nik said. "Your superpowers only work when your target is unaware of you. You're a key player in this event. He probably has a picture of you on his pinboard."

"Damn it! You're right."

Nik repeated his offer to spy on her sister's stalker. "He won't notice me. I'm just a guy."

In the suit he'd worn to dinner Friday night, which had hung in her closet all weekend, he was way more than "just a guy." He was one good-looking man. That said, he had a point: he was just another local businessman. There was no reason for Trick to suspect him.

"Alright, go!" She handed him his marching orders. "Keep your ears open. According to Ari, he chats up the locals and gets them talking."

"Will do," he said. "You stay here, under this awning, safe and out of sight."

"What are you worried about?" she asked. "He's not dangerous."

"You don't know that."

"Actually, I do." The guy was a content creator, not a serial killer. "Don't worry. I'll be safe."

Nik took off. Sasha had a camera with her this time around. It was a simple point-and-shoot with a better zoom lens than her phone—still not ideal. She snapped a few photos of Nik crossing the street. His swagger alone made her swoon.

She couldn't wait for this mission to be over with. Sasha was dying to see his apartment. She expected a generic space, but did it hold clues to his past life? He would love her place in California. It was small but full of light and plants. She loved its warm wood floors high archways and vintage bath with claw-foot tub. Her bedroom was a loft you couldn't stand upright in. Somehow, she didn't think Nik would mind.

Sticky ice cream dripping down her arm brought her back to reality. It occurred to her how ridiculous this plan was. She'd sent Nik on a fool's errand, and yet he was game. This man had her heart.

Trick exited the shop and strolled off in the opposite direction. Sasha snapped a photo, not sure what, if anything, she'd do with it.

Nik came out a moment later. Sasha snapped a few more photos for which she had very specific designs.

She held out the melting Popsicle. "I saved you the last of the ice cream."

"Thank you, honey." He finished it in one bite. "You won't believe what I found out."

It was too late to tell him that she no longer cared. If Ariana could shake off her obsession with this trickster, so could she. Except, he had her attention now and her curiosity had won out. "Tell me," she said.

Nik draped an arm over her shoulders and together they strolled along the sidewalk. "Trick… has heartburn."

"What?"

"It's a drugstore, Sasha. He bought over-the-counter antacid medication."

"That's it?"

"That's it."

"He didn't ask any questions?"

"Not while I was there."

"Well… Okay then."

"Are we done here?" he asked.

She nudged him in the ribs. "You're such a good sport."

"Anything for you," he said.

The way he said it made her want to believe it was true.

After the grand tour of Nik's one-bedroom apartment, she said, "How can you stand it? It's too generic. Nothing personal. Ari at least brought stuff from home for her rental. I miss my apartment. Don't you miss your place in Miami?"

He was scrolling his phone, about to order dinner. He looked up with a quizzical look on his face.

"Did I say something wrong?" Sasha asked.

He clammed up whenever she mentioned the sale of his condo, or at least he'd done so the one and only time he'd mentioned it. What was going on there?

Nik set his phone down on the coffee table and pulled her onto the oatmeal-colored couch. "We have to talk."

Oh, no. Sasha's stomach dropped. "What is it?"

"I was going to wait until after dinner."

Again, curiosity got the best of her. "Just tell me now!"

Nik folded into himself before her eyes. She reached out to him, grabbed him by the arms, and pulled him back. "Don't do that. Stay here with me."

"Oh, honey," he said. "What do you think I'm going to say?"

"I don't know! Just say it!"

"I plan on moving to California permanently by the end of the year. We're moving our LA office to Silicon Valley and I plan to be there full-time."

She was stunned. "What? Really?"

"Yes, really."

Huh… That was a startling revelation. "Are you familiar with California at all?" she asked.

"I fly in and out of Los Angeles every month, but I don't see more than the office and hotel."

"Okay," she proceeded sheepishly. "Silicon Valley is in the Bay Area, which is where I live."

His beautiful mouth twisted as he suppressed a smile. "I realize that."

"So…like…we'd be in the same geographic area."

"I figured that out, Sasha."

Sasha withdrew from him, dropping her hands onto her lap. "Why didn't you want to tell me?"

Nik swallowed hard. "Because it would be awkward."

"Awkward how?"

She could see his inner turmoil, but Sasha had to have these answers. Given the option, would he prefer not to go on seeing her? Had this already solidified as a temporary thing in his mind? She'd spent so much time wondering if she could commit to Nik, and no thought at all to if he even wanted a committed relationship. After all, he was moving to California for work. Maybe that was his first priority.

"I didn't want it to seem like I was taking over your turf."

Her turf? Seriously? It came down to turf wars?

"Sasha," he said, and took her hands. "I'm fumbling this. Let me start again."

Sasha waited while he collected his thoughts, her heart cracking with each passing second. How was it that she was already so invested in this?

"You made it clear this is just a fling."

"No," she said. "We never defined this, Nik."

His eyes went dark as he considered her words. "I'm just going to ask," he said. "Does it bother you that I'm moving to your city?"

Sasha shook her head. It truly didn't bother her. "I'd love to take you to my favorite restaurants."

Her answer didn't satisfy him. "I want to be clear about this," he said. "I don't need a tour guide around the city. I'd like to keep seeing you."

That was pretty clear! Sasha released all the air

trapped in her lungs. "Why didn't you just say that? Were you scared I'd scurry away?"

"Yes," he said, categorically. "I was scared."

In her linen blouse and cutoff shorts, Sasha wasn't dressed for seduction. She was going to attempt it anyway. She slipped off her top. "I'll make a few things clear. I like you, and I like how I feel around you. And no matter what you say, I'm taking you on a tour of my city. If you think you can stop me—"

Nik cupped her face and kissed her hard. She leaned back against the cushions and drew him on top of her. Then she changed her mind and pushed him off. "Not here! We've already done it on a couch," she explained. "We should try something new."

"The shower?" he suggested.

She glared at him. "Did you forget this morning already?"

"Does that really count?"

Arguably, it didn't. They'd kissed until the water ran cold.

"That only leaves the kitchen," Nik said, his voice husky with desire. "And we both think that's overrated."

"True."

"What's the issue?" he asked. "We don't have to tik every box right away We've got time."

They had time. There was no rush, no hard and fast deadline. Nik was coming to San Francisco. He would see her charming apartment, and he'd love it. They'd go for authentic dim sum in Chinatown. They'd get to know each other slowly. She would open her life and make room for him. This was not the beginning, middle and end. She could dim the fire to a slow simmer.

"I've been rushing this because I thought it would be over soon," she said. "I wanted to experience everything, make sure we left nothing on the table."

Nik pressed his forehead to hers. "I can promise you this—we're not leaving anything on the table."

Sasha kissed him, her tongue sweeping and exploring his mouth. When she pulled away, breathless, her gaze slid to the dining table.

"Don't even think about it," Nik said. "That thing is basically particleboard. It'll break."

Dinner was pizza eaten out of the carton. They sat on scattered pillows and drank wine and talked into the night.

Nik told her about a conversation with his cousin. She'd cashed in her 401K to pay for art classes in Europe. "I want to help her out. I know she won't let me. She's so stubborn."

"Financially, you mean. Otherwise, she has it in hand."

"Yeah." Nik set aside his plate and rested his head on Sasha's lap. "She shouldn't go broke to pursue her dream."

Sasha wiped her hands on the paper-thin napkins and cradled Nik's face between her palms. "You're going to have to get creative. Ariana helped me out those early days. One Christmas, she paid my rent for a year. I made a fuss, but I would've been a fool to turn it down. I wouldn't be where I am now without her help. I was able to leave my hometown at a time that I desperately needed to, and take an unpaid internship in one of the most expensive cities in the country. Six months later, I had a job."

"Why were you desperate to leave your hometown?" he asked.

Sasha shrugged. "You're missing the point of the story."

Nik traced the curve of her jawline with a tip of a finger. "Why were you desperate, Sasha?"

She caught his hand and pressed a kiss to the back of it. They were talking about his cousin and her issues. There was no need to stir up all this.

A crinkle appeared between his brows. "Was this right after the wedding?"

"The canceled wedding, you mean?"

Nik said nothing. Somehow, his silence added weight to her question. She blinked back fresh tears. "It was a difficult year," she said. "I lost friends. Nothing dramatic, obviously, it was an awkward situation all around. Some pitied me. Others picked sides. I was alone a lot. I felt left out. Leaving San Bernardino was the best decision I ever made."

Nik sat up and looked at her a long time. "I don't ever want you to feel that lonely again."

He said it as if he could decide her fate. "One can only hope," she said. "Anyway, I'm in a good place now."

He eased her back onto a bed of pillows and crawled over her. "Here with me, you mean?"

Sasha let out a small laugh. "I meant in life in general, but sure."

"May I make love to you here? Or is it not innovative enough?"

"It's fine." She wrapped her legs around his. "You can make love to me on the rooftop later on."

He kissed the hollow of her neck. "Deal."

Sometime in the night, they made love in Nik's soft bed. He parted her knees, and Sasha lost all sense of time to the stroke of his tongue and the scrape of his scruff on her thighs. When he went away to find a condom, she felt a sense of loss so deep, she had to call out his name. "I'm not going anywhere," he tried to reassure her, but words were not enough. She wasn't satisfied until he was deep inside her, his breath fanning her cheek, his voice in her ear coaxing her to surrender to him.

Sasha didn't need coaxing. She was already in his power.

Nineteen

Back at the hotel the next morning, Sasha poured a cup of coffee and caught up on some editing. Watching Nik whirl around his apartment, prepping for a busy day while taking calls from Oliver, was enough to make her miss work, or at least the sense of purpose that came with every new assignment. She decided to pitch the smokehouse story to the editor of *Table for Two*, a culinary magazine.

Sasha shifted through the images of Donna's kitchen, the old barn and the surrounding fields. She came across the one photo she'd taken of Nik. He sat with his elbows on the table; his golden-brown eyes gleamed in the sun. It was hard to believe that he was practically a stranger then. And yet, she'd snapped that photo only minutes before they'd kissed. In such a short time, he'd done so much to make her life beautiful, to make her feel safe. He was so concerned for her well-being that he was willing to put her interests above his own, rethinking a move to California.

What had she done for him in return? Not much.

It was time to correct that.

This morning, while getting dressed, she overheard Nik on the phone with Oliver, discussing yet another failed attempt at a meeting with the CEO of Mad Dash. She went into the bathroom to gather her braids into a high ponytail when she heard Nik admit that he was ready to give up. That didn't sit well with her.

She exited the photo-editing app and logged into her social media account. She had no trouble finding Teresa Price; they had ten friends in common. Sasha composed a quick direct message, asking if they could talk. In the subject line, she wrote: I need a favor. There was no use playing around. She didn't want to catch up or talk about old times. She wouldn't propose they meet for coffee. A straightforward request would catch Teresa's attention. She would not miss the opportunity to show off.

Sasha was right. Before she'd finished up with her photo edits, Teresa had messaged her back: Video chat?

Sasha's hands fell away from the laptop keyboard. It was ridiculous how a chance encounter with one of her ex-fiancé's many cousins at an airport or the prospect of a video call with an old friend of his could cause so much inner turmoil. She was not going to spend the rest of her life punishing herself for letting Terrence down, for choosing her happiness over his. Underneath the grief, she was thankful to her former self for having the courage to walk away. She loved her life and now she'd found a person who wanted to be in it as it was. That was what this video call was all about.

Even so, she had to look good. Sasha let down her braids and swiped on lipstick. A moment later, she was face-to-face with Teresa, a dark-eyed brunette with a soft round face and the pointy teeth of a predator.

"Sasha!" she cried. "Long time no see!"

Terrence and Teresa were "TNT" to the group. Sasha prepared herself to be detonated.

"I know!" Sasha said. "Wild, right?"

"How have you been?" she asked with a tone that fell just short of condescension.

Sasha held an even smile. "I'm doing great. Thanks."

"I might have come across one of a photo of you in a magazine, but I can't say for sure."

She didn't work for tabloids, so the chances of Teresa coming across her work were slim. "I'm published widely, so it's possible."

"Not one of your photos," she said. "A photograph of you leaving a restaurant in Texas on the arm of a striking man."

Ah…well…one way or the other, she'd landed in the tabloids. "Yup. That was me. I plead guilty."

"There's a lot of talk surrounding your sister's wedding. Can you believe it?"

"It's to be expected. Ari and Ex *are* the power couple of the moment."

"If this wedding even happens."

The knives were out. "Stay tuned!"

Teresa checked her watch. "I'm short on time. You said you needed a favor."

"Yes, I do," Sasha said, eager to get off the call herself. "Ari tells me you're the CFO of Mad Dash."

"Oh my God! She knows about that?"

"She's a customer. She loves the service."

"Wow!" Teresa exclaimed. "Would she be willing to endorse us?"

"No." Sasha was firm on that. She was accustomed to dodging these types of requests. "I'm here on behalf of the striking man in the photo."

Teresa leaned in toward the screen. "Really?"

"His name in Nikolai Williams," Sasha said. "His PR firm, Nexus, wants a meeting with Mad Dash. They handle Xavier Noble's account, and he couldn't be happier."

"Really?"

"Yes, really."

"Hmm… Obviously, I can't say yes or no, right now on the spot."

"I understand," Sasha said. "Look up the firm, and give it some thought. If you're interested, contact the firm directly. I'll stay out of it from here on out."

"Sounds fair," Teresa said. "I'll tell you this. If they're good enough for Xavier Noble, they should be good enough for our little start-up."

"According to Forbes, there's nothing little about your start-up."

Teresa cackled. "Who am I to argue with Forbes?"

It was time to pull the plug. "Thanks for your time. I know you're busy."

"We'll keep in touch, Sasha!" Teresa said, all smiles. "Don't be a stranger."

Sasha exited the video chat and fell back into her chair. The five-minute conversation left her depleted. Who knew name-dropping required so much energy? All in all, it was the right thing to do. Nik worked so hard. He deserved a break.

A calendar alert popped on the computer screen. She had an appointment with her therapist in *five* minutes. Sasha had forgotten all about it. Crap! What was there to report? She was happy and doing well for the first time ever. But it was too late to cancel. She poured herself another cup of coffee and got settled for the half-hour session.

It began in the usual way. After polite greetings, her therapist read from his notes. "The last time we spoke, your sister's wedding was coming up. You had some anxiety about that. It exposed some unhealed trauma. You should be in Texas now. How's it going?"

Her therapist was a middle-aged man named

Jonas Bradford. There were times Sasha wished she'd gone with a woman therapist. Dr. Jonas could be quite dry, and she would have preferred a chattier approach to therapy. However, Dr. Jonas came highly recommended and Ariana pointed out that her expectation of a chatty, sassy woman therapist was sexist. "She's not your bestie."

"It's going great," Sasha said.

"Good to hear," Dr. Jonas said. "Tell me more."

"I met someone," she said. "He's perfect."

Dr. Jonas stared back at her from over the rim of his drugstore reading glasses. He'd mentioned he bought them in bulk. "When did you meet this person?"

"On the flight to Royal," Sasha said. "His name is Nik."

Dr. Jonas started scribbling furiously on his digital notepad. Sasha waited patiently. "It's Nik with a K."

He crossed out a word and rewrote it.

"He does business in Texas, but soon he'll be settling down near me to run their West Coast office. Isn't that awesome?"

The look Dr. Jonas gave her made it clear he didn't think it was awesome at all. "Are you comfortable with the pace at which this new relationship is advancing?"

"I am," Sasha said. "When you know, you know."

The Harvard-trained psychologist could hardly hide his skepticism. "Let's analyze this more deeply, shall we?"

Sasha twisted in her seat. "Okay."

"It is worth noting that you are starting something new mere weeks before a triggering event."

She preferred not to think of her only sister's wedding as a triggering event; still, she understood where he was coming from.

"I agree the timing isn't ideal," Sasha said. "But Nik is so wonderful. He put all my fears to rest."

"There is no ideal timing," Dr. Jonas said. "However, there are advantages to taking it slow. You may want to check on how you feel about him when your sister's wedding is over and done, and you're back to your everyday life."

"You think I'm clinging to Nik like a life raft to avoid drowning in my feelings," Sasha said.

"Those are your words," Dr. Jonas said. "Nonetheless, it's a theory worth exploring."

Long after the session was over, Sasha sat staring at her blank computer screen. *Those are your words...* Was she moving this fast with Nik as a way to prove to Ariana and herself that she was over the past? Was she using him? The answer erupted violently inside her.

NO!

Every time he touched her, every look they shared, she had all the confirmation she needed. Yes, she was going through some things. *Nonetheless*, Nik was worth holding onto, particularly in times of great turbulence. She had no intention of letting him go or slowing things down or anything else. If this plane was crashing down, she was going down with it.

Twenty

After an exceptional lunch meeting with a client, Oliver and Nik stayed behind at the restaurant to toast their accomplishment.

"I'll have a whisky neat," Nik said to the waiter.

"Me, too," Oliver said. "It's five o'clock somewhere."

"This is Texas," the waiter replied. "You don't have to rationalize it."

When the whiskies arrived, they toasted to Nexus and Texas.

"It's been twenty-four hours," Oliver said. "It's time for a status report. Are you still in love or was that a passing feeling?"

Nik swirled his glass. "Still in love. Can't shake it."

"Does Sasha know how you feel?" Oliver asked.

"Not yet."

"I know how you feel before she does?" Oliver folded over with laughter. "Man! We're close, but you're taking this too far!"

"I've made some progress. I told her about the move to California."

"And? How did she take it?"

Nik relived the moment. Either he'd done a poor job expressing himself or she'd misread him completely. Either way, he saw the pain and confusion in her eyes. He felt like the biggest jerk then. She deserved honesty. In the end, his fears were unfounded.

"She was amazing about it. She wants to show me around."

"See?" Oliver grinned like the know-it-all he was. "It was all in your head. Now go tell her that you love her."

"We're not there yet."

"How do you know?" Oliver asked. "If you feel so strongly, there's a good chance she feels the same."

Nik doubted it. Sasha had his head spinning at hello. "There's no rush," he said. "We have time."

Right then, both their phones buzzed with messages. Their accounts manager, Daria, had messaged them both in all caps: TERESA PRICE, CFO OF MAD DASH, HAS REQUESTED A MEETING. WHAT SAY YOU GUYS?

Oliver barked out a laugh and started typing right away. WE SAY: HELL YEAH! ANYTIME.

Nik couldn't wrap his mind around it. His every lead had gone stale. "I don't get it," he said. "Why now?"

"I get it," Oliver said. "You did the work. You wore them down. And now we have one more thing to toast to." He raised his glass. "Good job, man! Here's to you!"

Although the victory didn't feel earned, Nik raised his glass. "To us!"

They met at the TCC. After much fawning over Ari and Ex, the mixologist got to the point and proposed a signature mocktail. "It is thoughtful to accommodate everyone."

Ariana agreed. "Of course."

Sasha nodded and kept on sipping the pineapple-based beverage.

When the mixologist offered a tour of the wine cellar where the TCC allowed them storage space for the wedding, Xavier leaped at the chance. Ari rested a hand on Sasha's shoulder and pinned her down on the barstool. "We'll stay here."

Her tone made it clear that Sasha did not have a choice.

Sasha mumbled into her glass, "Fine with me."

Once the men were out of earshot, Ariana's grip turned tighter. "What's wrong?"

Sasha winced. "What do you mean?"

"You've been sulking all afternoon," she said. "This is the fun errand! You had more fun at the dress shop yesterday and you hate shopping."

"I'm sorry." Sasha slumped over the polished mahogany bar.

"Don't be sorry. Tell me what's wrong. Is it…" Ari hesitated. "Is it Nik? Did you two have a falling-out?"

Sasha could have drowned in her mocktail at the mention of his name. "Can I get something stronger?"

Ariana reached for a bottle of gin left on the bar and topped off her glass. "Talk. What did he do?"

"He did nothing!"

"He did *something*."

Sasha swiveled in her seat to face her sister. It was time to come clean. "I have something to confess. Nik and I have grown closer these past few days."

Ari topped off her own glass. "Who are you telling? I've witnessed this *closeness*."

"He plans to move to the Bay Area in a few months for its proximity to Silicon Valley. That's the next frontier for Nexus."

"How exciting!" Ari cried. "Is that why you're freaking out?"

"Not at all." It was the opposite: she was elated. This was the best thing that could happen. She and Nik had time on their side now. "I spoke to my therapist today."

"And you told him you're making healthy choices," Ari supplied.

Well, not quite. "He thinks the timing of this blossoming friendship is suspect. He thinks that I may be using Nik as a distraction to avoid dealing with the issues your wedding brought up."

"What do you think?" Ari asked.

"I think he thinks the same thing *you* thought," Sasha retorted.

"I have no reason to think that way now that

he's moving to the Bay Area," Ari said. "There's a path forward. Whatever is *blossoming* can take root."

Sasha rolled her eyes. So many metaphors to skirt the truth! "I have to wonder if he's right. I was nervous about this trip and what did I do? I latched on to the first man I locked eyes with even before the plane landed."

"In this case, the plane didn't land as much as it skidded to a stop," Ari said. "What choice did you have?"

"None, really."

"It's serendipity or whatever."

"Is that even a real thing?" Sasha said, skeptical.

Ari was having none of it. "That's rich coming from a woman who believes in curses."

She had a point there.

"If it weren't for my wedding, you likely wouldn't have started therapy. If it weren't for my wedding, you wouldn't have traveled to Royal at all. And, lastly, if it weren't for my wedding, you might have never met Nik."

"Right! This is all *your* fault."

"Ha ha!" she said dryly. "I'm serious, Sasha."

"So am I!" Sasha wailed. "That's what I'm trying to tell you. I'm serious about Nik. He's stirred up so many feelings..."

Ari was at the edge of her seat. "You have feelings?"

Sasha let out a breath. "Yes," she said. "I have feelings for Nik."

"Whew!" Ari mimed wiping sweat off her brow. "I had to work for that one."

"What are you talking about?"

"It was obvious to me from the start that you liked him," Ari said. "You lit up when he walked through the door. I didn't want you to mess it up. So you can report back to your therapist that I took the necessary steps to force you to examine your feelings."

"Thank you, Dr. Ramos."

Ari flashed a cocky little smile. "You're welcome."

"So...you don't think we're moving too fast?" Sasha asked sheepishly.

"Not unless you think so," Ari said.

"I do, absolutely," Sasha said. "But I like where things are headed."

"Well then, this calls for a toast." Ari raised her glass. "To new beginnings!"

Sasha didn't have it in her to say that she and

Nik had sprinted far past the starting line. She fixed a smile on her face and raised her glass. “To new beginnings!”

Twenty-One

Good luck with your meeting!

Nik received the text message five minutes before they were scheduled to start. A smile crept on his face as he typed a response: Why do I need luck? I have you.

He hadn't seen her in two days. Ever since Teresa Price of Mad Dash had requested a meeting, it was all hands on deck for the team. Long days spent at the office, no time for lunch breaks, eating dinner out of takeout containers—that was their standard operational procedure. Signing Mad Dash wouldn't make or break Nexus; they'd had a banner year. However, this was the sort of energy they brought to any deal. They went in hot.

He and Sasha still managed to talk every night. When he explained the situation to her, she was supportive. She was gleeful, even. He felt more than lucky to have her in his life.

Presently, they were all in the conference room. With a few clicks, they initiated the video call. Teresa Price appeared on the wall-mounted monitor.

"Good evening!" she said brightly. "Or good afternoon! Forgive me. I don't know what time it is over there."

They exchanged pleasantries, discussed the weather and finally got down to business. Nik started with their usual opening: "Today we want to persuade you to switch teams and take a chance with us."

"It wouldn't be a risk," Teresa said. "Isn't it true you handle Xavier Noble's PR?"

Considering that Xavier was trending on all social media platforms at the moment, Nik didn't consider this answer odd.

"Xavier Noble is one of our newest clients," Oliver said. "He's a novelist with specific goals for his career."

"Mad Dash is shaping how commerce is done in the United States and we want to help you make an impact," Nik added.

"I'm listening," Teresa said.

Nik went on to present a brief overview of Mad Dash's current state of affairs and the markets in which it could potentially grow. "You fare better in sprawling suburban areas with aging populations, places where quick trips to a convenience store or the shoe repair shop becomes a hassle for the elderly or the disabled. Texas has its big cities, of course, but there are a great many communities, such as Royal, where your services could benefit the population. It's about micro-targeting."

"Micro-targeting, that sounds smart," Teresa said. "May I ask you a question?"

"Of course," Nik replied. "Interrupt me at any time."

"Are you Sasha Ramos's new boyfriend?"

Was he…what?

Nik didn't know what to say. Aside from the fact that his relationship status wasn't this woman's business, he wasn't comfortable presenting himself as Sasha's boyfriend. They hadn't had that talk yet.

"You're the man in the photo, right? The one in all the magazines?"

Nik was aware that the photo of him and Sasha leaving Sheen had made the tabloid rounds. He didn't expect it to come up five minutes into his presentation.

Oliver tossed him a glance, letting him know that he could handle Teresa's questions any way he liked.

"That was me," he said. "Sasha is a friend."

Teresa's smile exposed a row of pointy teeth. "That was rude of me," she said. "I didn't mean to interrupt your presentation. Continue."

Thick silence weaved through the room. Oliver cut through it by clearing his throat. He went on to point out the various markets in which Mad Dash had the most potential for growth in Texas. "Once you've covered these areas, it'll only be a matter of time before the city dwellers start clamoring for your services," Oliver concluded. "You know how much they hate to be left out."

They all laughed. The mood lightened somewhat until Teresa brought it crashing down.

"Sasha—"

"What?" Nik interrupted. If they could conclude this meeting without bringing up Sasha, he would be grateful.

"*Sasha,*" she repeated with bloody satisfaction, "highly recommended you."

"You spoke to Sasha about us?"

"Yes," Teresa said with a rolling laugh. "I should have mentioned it at the top. She's an old friend. She recommended I take this meeting. I like what I'm hearing so far. It all sounds great. It just doesn't sound great *enough.* What else do you bring to the table?"

At this point, Oliver had to take over the meeting. Nik was too astonished to behave professionally. He was furious with this woman who was clearly here to toy with them. To a degree less, he was angry with Sasha for putting them in this situation. She had never shown any interest in his business beyond offering general support and encouragement, and here she was reaching out to old friends and setting up meetings. He thought of her text. Good luck with the meeting. It blew his mind. Good luck with the meeting that she'd arranged?

"With Nexus you get a team dedicated to building sustainable growth," Oliver said.

"That's what they all say," Teresa said with a slight roll of her eyes.

"We know you're interested in Texas," Nik cut in. "But Texas is not a monolith. We see the potential of Mad Dash becoming an essential resource in communities with the most need. It's a smarter and more cost-effective approach than blanketing the state of Texas in a hit-or-miss fashion. But if you'd rather talk about my girlfriend—"

"Don't get testy!" Teresa said. "I'm a business-woman first—I had to push your buttons. I heard what you had to say and I'll take it back to the team. They'll probably want to meet with you, too. For the moment, our CEO is out of town and can't be reached so it'll have to wait."

"That's all we ask," Oliver said. "Thanks for meeting with us."

"You're welcome," Teresa said. "I'll be honest. I only agreed to this in the hopes of scoring a last-minute invite to the *royal wedding* of our times. I'm obsessed with the story! I knew Ariana before she was famous. We're all from San Bernardino. That said, you made some valid points. If we want to conquer Texas, so to speak, it would be wise to partner with a company with boots on the ground. We'll be in touch."

The monitor screen went dark. Oliver gave Nik a blank stare. "What the hell was that?"

Nik snapped shut his notebook. "I have no idea," he said through clenched teeth.

"Did Sasha mention—"

"No, she did *not*."

"Hold on," Oliver said. "She had to have done it in good faith. Anyway, we killed it. So, kudos to her! We probably wouldn't have gotten a meeting otherwise."

Nik wasn't willing to go that far. "Yes, but—"

"I know," Oliver said. "You were blindsided, and it's not cool."

"It's not cool!" Nik repeated hotly. After all the work he'd put into preparing, to be thrown off like that, unnecessarily. They'd talked every night. She'd had ample opportunity to clue him in.

"No argument here," Oliver said.

Nik rose from the table and collected his things. He had to talk to her.

"Where are you going?" Oliver asked.

"Where do you think?"

"I think you should go home, go on a run,

whatever, just cool off before you speak with her. Turn off your phone, if that helps," Oliver said. "That's my advice. Take it for what it's worth."

Nik turned off his phone. "Going dark."

Oliver called out to him just when he reached the conference room door. "Hey! One last thing."

"What's that?"

"You called Sasha your girlfriend earlier."

"I did?"

Oliver grinned. "Yep, it's official!"

For once, they were staying in. Sasha was spending the evening at her sister's place. Ari was puttering about in her favorite faded jeans. She'd lit a fragrant candle and put on a jazz record. Ex was in the other room, revising an article he'd written for a popular men's magazine. Sasha sat at the marble dinner table, sifting through a collection of ribbons for the perfect shade of bluebonnet blue.

She held up a short ribbon for Ari to inspect. "How about this?"

"Mmm… Too light."

She held up another. "And this?"

"Too dark."

"Oh, God!" Sasha muttered.

"Just keep looking!" Ari insisted. "Bluebonnet blue is a specific color. That first one was more turquoise than anything else."

"Bluebonnets come in pink, purple and white. Look it up."

Ari switched the record. "That's not helpful."

Sasha went on sifting.

In the best of times, her heart wouldn't be in the task, but she hadn't heard from Nik, not since his last and very sweet text message: Why do I need luck? I have you.

She'd been all day waiting for an update. Her calls went straight to voice mail. Either he'd turned off his phone in preparation for the meeting and forgot to turn it back on, or he was too busy with follow-up work. That didn't change the fact that she hadn't seen him in two days, and was starting to forget the taste of his kiss.

It took a half hour, but she finally sold Ari on ribbon the color of cornflower.

After a quiet dinner, Sasha turned down Ex's offer for a ride. It was a crisp night and she preferred to walk to her hotel. "It's only a few blocks," she assured them, adding a hug for good measure. "I could use the fresh air."

It had been a struggle keeping her mood even

at her sister's place. Sasha was not one to hide her feelings; they were always projected onto her face. She didn't want Ari to suspect anything was amiss with Nik, not that anything was amiss. He was busy with work, work generated from a meeting that she'd arranged. It was her damn fault, and now she was paying for it.

Back at the hotel, while waiting for an elevator, she checked her phone one last time. Nothing. She dropped the phone into her wicker tote. An elevator car opened and a sea of people poured out, Nik among them. Just like that, the gloomy clouds that had followed her around all afternoon dissipated.

Sasha rushed to him and with a hand to his chest, guided him back into the elevator. The doors closed and they were alone. "Where have you been? Why didn't you call?"

"I wanted to talk to you in person," he said.

"Well, here I am," she said. "I've missed you!"

She grabbed his tie and pulled him into a kiss. Hand to her heart, she swore Nik hesitated before he kissed her back. She then promptly forgot all about it when his hands gripped her bottom and pulled her into him.

Two days of separation was too much. They

tore at each other, their hands roaming freely, and violently pulled apart when the elevator stopped on a random floor. She swiveled around and smoothed down her minidress. Nik leaned against the handrail and held her close with a hand on her hip. She could feel him hard against her lower back.

The doors slid open, achingly slow. An elderly woman asked, "Going down?"

"No," Sasha answered. "Definitely going up."

"Thanks," the woman said. "Have a good night."

"You, too."

The doors inched shut. Sasha fell onto Nik's chest. He swept her braids aside and slid a hot kiss down her neck. She moaned and reached out blindly for his free hand and placed it over her breast. Nik had other designs. He gathered the hem of her dress and—

They'd reached her floor. The doors slid opened, and they stumbled out. Sasha grabbed his arm and tugged him in the direction of her suite. In a gesture that she found sexy, he slipped out her key card and waved them in.

The door hadn't clicked shut and she was out of her dress. The white linen shift lay crumpled on the floor. Nik tore off his clothes, scooped her up and carried her into…the kitchen.

So, they were doing this.

He lifted her onto the counter and took care of the condom. The wait was making her mad. *"Hurry!"*

Nik looked up at her, his eyes dark. "You're going to be the end of me."

She wrapped her legs around his waist. "Let's find out."

He sunk inside her. Sasha closed her eyes. The commotion inside her quieted, and roared back up again. Nik controlled the pace, ignoring her pleas. He would not let her rush their pleasure. It was worth the exquisite torture when they unraveled together.

Moments later, they were on the kitchen floor drinking from the bottle of wine that Nik had brought that first night. Sasha pressed the back of her hand to his cheek. "How did the meeting go?"

He met her eyes, and did not answer.

It dawned on her then that Nik hadn't uttered more than a few words to her all day. "Is something wrong?" she asked.

"Why didn't you tell me you set up the meeting?" he said.

"Oh…" Sasha's stomach turned. "That…"

She pulled herself up off the floor. "Let's go to the couch. It's more comfortable over there."

She was stalling for time. Why *hadn't* she told him? When he framed it that way, it seemed deceitful. It wasn't her intention to mislead him. She'd wanted to do something nice for him, and that was what she came up with.

Nik rolled onto his feet. It stung her when he stopped to pull on his pants before joining her on the couch. Feeling exposed, she went into her bathroom and slipped on a robe. When she got back, he had his shirt on. It was unbuttoned and loose over his sculpted chest, but still. Was he planning on leaving?

Sasha knew she'd better clear the air. She stood before him, her hands in her pockets. "It was meant to be a surprise. I wanted to do something nice to make up for everything that I'd put you through. When you brought up Mad Dash over dinner, Ariana pointed out that an old friend of mine was the company's CFO. I got the idea that maybe I could put in a good word for you."

Nik's face remained stone hard. Sasha eased

onto the couch next to him. "Did the meeting not go well?"

"It started with Teresa Price asking if I was your boyfriend and ended with her angling for a wedding invitation," Nik said. "It didn't go great."

Sasha was shocked. "I'm sorry. I thought she'd be more professional than that."

"She wasn't professional at all," Nik said. "I don't see how you two could have ever been friends."

"She was Terrence's friend, to be honest."

He scrunched his brows. "Terrence?"

"My ex-fiancé," Sasha said with a sigh. "Teresa and Terrence went to business school together. They were TNT."

Nik blinked at her, unmoved, leading Sasha to think that in life, like in sitcoms, a laugh track was useful. She threw her hands up in exasperation. "That was a joke, by the way!"

"I get the joke," he said evenly. "Here's what I don't understand. You reached out to your ex-fiancé's college buddy to help me out?"

"Yes!"

"And you did it to 'make up for everything' you'd put me through?"

"Exactly!"

"What exactly did you put me through?"

"All of it!" she cried, although she was hard pressed to come up with a single example. "The ride from the airport, for one thing."

"That was my pleasure, Sasha," he said. "I was more than happy to do it."

"Even so, you could have had a quiet, pleasant ride without me there talking up a storm and driving you to distraction."

"Do you think I wanted quiet and pleasant?" he asked.

This discussion was going off the rails. "Nik, can't a person do one nice thing for you? I'm sorry the meeting didn't go well, but you have to believe it wasn't my intention. I wasn't trying to set you up."

Nik wasn't listening to her. "You said your fiancé's friends shunned you after the breakup."

"They did," she said, wearily. "Teresa chief among them."

"And you reached out to her anyway?" Nik dropped his elbows onto his knees. "Why would you think I'd want that?"

"To sign the company!" Sasha was beyond exasperated now. "Isn't that what you business people do?"

"God, Sasha!" Nik was clearly beyond exasperated, as well. "I'd rather walk away from any deal than have you put yourself in that position."

Deep inside, Sasha understood why he was upset. Reaching out to Teresa had left a bad taste in her mouth. It was icky, to say the least. That was probably why she hadn't told him.

"You put yourself though that, meanwhile I'm not sure I want to do business with them," he said. "As much as I think this company has potential, I don't know that the people running it are serious. I've been chasing after them for weeks. It took you pulling strings to get in touch with them at all. The CEO is MIA and the CFO is more interested in a wedding invite than a business plan."

Sasha listened and nodded. "I understand. You're under no obligation to move forward, not on my account."

"Don't reach out to her again," he said. "She's not a good person."

"I know that now," Sasha said. "Please don't scold me."

"I'm not—"

Nik stopped and let out a breath. Next thing, he was on his feet and working on the buttons of his shirt. Sasha watched him wordlessly. Anger and annoyance shot through her. "Are you leaving?"

His hands dropped to his side. "I don't want to fight. It's been a long day, and I'm fried. It's best we cool off tonight."

If Nik Williams thought he'd come by, make love to her on her kitchen counter, drink her wine, accuse her of meddling in his career and take off, well…fine! She wasn't going to stop him. In fact, she would escort him to the door.

"I spoke to Jonas about us. He thinks we're rushing it."

Nik took a step back. "Who is Jonas?"

"My therapist!" she spat. Why she'd weaponized the word was anyone's guess.

"You told your therapist about me?" he asked.

"I did, and he thinks we're taking this too far," Sasha said. "I'm starting to think he's right."

Nik ran a hand through his hair. "Because we're having a disagreement?"

"Because you don't know me!" she shouted. "This is just who I am. I rush into things, realize my mistake way too late, and back out at the last second."

"What are we even talking about?" Nik asked. "Are we still talking about Teresa Price?"

"We're talking about everything!" she kept on shouting. A small voice in her back of her mind was saying: *Don't do this! Settle down, calm down, come back to this with a cool head.* She muted that voice. "And for the record, this is not a *disagreement*. This is a fight, and you're not going to win."

Shock, hurt and anger projected onto his face. To her horror, Sasha realized that she was the villain here. She'd created the problem, aggravated the problem, and now she was going to compound it by theatrically pointing to the door and ordering him to leave. "Good night, Nik."

He walked past her. She sank deeper into the couch, arms folded, listening while he looked around for his shoes and belt. After ordering him to go, she couldn't beg him to stay. That was a bit much, even for her. Yet she didn't want him to walk out like this. If they could keep talking, they could resolve this.

"I have a question," he said.

Sasha was immediately on her feet. "What is it?"

He was wrapping his tie around his fist. Nik

didn't usually wear ties. He'd likely pulled all the stops for the train wreck of a meeting she'd set up.

"First it was your sister who didn't want us to jump into anything, now it's your therapist," he said. "When are you going to admit that it's you?"

Sasha took a step back as the chances of her winning this fight were waning.

"You don't think we should be together," he continued. "You think we're moving too fast, and you don't have to hide behind the opinions of others. You can just say what you're thinking yourself."

"I'm perfectly capable of speaking up for myself, Nik," she retorted. "You should know that by now."

"Here's what I know," he said. "You're a spontaneous person. I love that about you. What you did this week was far from spontaneous. You planned this. You placed the call to your former fiancé's friend. You held your tongue for two days while I was busy prepping for the meeting you set up. This was not a spontaneous gesture. It was a decision on your part."

Sasha charged forward. "Are you done?"

"No, I have one last thing to get off my chest."

"What is it?"

"I'm not convinced you went through this trouble for me."

"Why else would I have done this?"

Sasha was shouting again. She couldn't help it. He had pushed every button there was to push. Maybe he did know her, after all.

"To get back in touch with your fiancé, or at least his friends." He shoved his tie in his pocket. "I never considered the fact that maybe you're not over him. Maybe the reason you can't move on is because you love him."

"If I loved him, I would have married him, don't you think?"

"Not if you believe you're cursed."

"Get out!" she hollered. "GET OUT!"

Nik's eyes clouded with sorrow, but he did what he was told. He set his key card on the console table on his way out the door.

Twenty-Two

Of all the ways to crash down to earth…

Sasha took another swig from the warm wine bottle. It was one in the morning and she still had a lot of fight in her. If anyone were spying on her through the hotel window, they'd catch a glimpse of a disheveled woman, pacing around in circles, drinking from a bottle and talking gibberish to herself.

Nik, her protector, her knight in shining armor, had betrayed her. That was the only way to put it. He'd *betrayed* her trust. She couldn't wrap her mind around it. How could she have so misjudged the man? He thought he wasn't over Terrence? Ha! Just wait until she showed him how fast she could get over him! She snapped her fingers. “Like that!” So fast, his head would spin.

Why is the room spinning?

If anything, this was confirmation that they’d jumped into something prematurely. What was she thinking? She’d meet a handsome stranger on a plane, fall in love and live happily ever after like in a freaking fairy tale?

Why is my head is splitting in two?

Seriously, though, what was she thinking? She and Nik were strangers swept up by adventure. There was no other explanation. It was all fun and games until things got real.

Sasha wandered into the bedroom and plopped onto the bed. The wine bottle landed with a thump on the rug.

Why is my heart breaking?

The next day, those questions plagued her still. She’d nursed the dull ache in her chest with antacid chewables with no success. At least she was out of bed, on her couch with a cup of coffee, binge-watching videos, her phone clutched in one hand—just in case.

Who knew how long she’d carry on like this if it weren’t for Ariana’s timely intervention. She banged on her door so forcefully, for a second there Sasha thought it was the local SWAT team. Ironic, considering that *she* was the real victim here.

"Hold on!" she cried.

Sasha wrapped the robe tighter around her body and puttered to the door. She opened without hesitation. It could only be one person.

Ariana jumped back, recoiling at her appearance. "My God, Sasha! What happened to you?"

"Come in, and keep quiet."

It was silly of her to think Ari could ever keep quiet. She stormed in, assessed the mess, and tossed her designer purse onto the one clear surface.

"Why haven't you answered my texts? We're going to the stationery store to pick out thank-you cards."

"Sorry, I'm falling to pieces at the moment," Sasha said. "I'll pass today."

"What's going on?"

"It's over between Nik and me," she said. "And I'm a mess."

As soon as she said the words, the dull ache in her chest lifted. It was as if the truth had been clawing to come out all this time. *It's over. I'm a mess.*

"When did this happen?" Ari asked. "You were fine yesterday."

Sasha plopped onto the couch. "What a difference a day makes."

Ari sat next to her. "Start from the beginning."

She couldn't if she tried. There was no beginning, middle or end. It was as if a bomb had detonated and blew her heart into smithereens. If she had to start somewhere, she might as well start with Teresa Price.

Ariana listened, and grimaced.

"Is it really that bad?" Sasha asked. "I had the best intentions."

"Ex and I have an agreement—we don't meddle or interfere in each other's careers. We don't offer unsolicited advice. How would you like it if I called in favors to get you jobs?"

Sasha wouldn't like it one bit.

"Still, that doesn't excuse Teresa," Ari said. "Who knew she could be such a bitch?"

Sasha raised a hand. "I did."

Ari whipped out her phone. "You know what? I'm deleting her app."

"No, don't do that!"

"It's done," she said, and pocketed the phone. "Is that all, or is there more to this?"

They hadn't even scratched the surface. "Nik thinks I'm not over Terrence."

"That's ridiculous," Ari said. "The whole family is over Terrence. We've moved on. What gave him that idea?"

"The way I keep strumming my pain and guilt over the way things ended," Sasha said. "That might have something to do with it."

Ari pondered this a while. "He may have a point there."

"Ari!" Sasha cried with indignation. "Don't you dare take his side!"

"Calm down," Ari said. "He's not here, so we can talk about it. He has a point. It's past time you move on. The man is engaged, for Christ's sake."

"What?"

It was a good thing Sasha was sitting down, because her ass would have hit the floor. "Are you kidding me?"

Ari blinked at her. "Why would I kid? And why don't you know these things? Don't you keep in touch with anyone?"

"I don't."

After she left San Bernardino, she'd deleted and blocked old contacts. She'd wanted a fresh start.

"Why not?" Ari asked. "I would be nowhere without Dee and—"

"You forget my friends were Terrence's friends, too," Sasha said. "We didn't part ways in the best of terms."

"Oh, sweetie…" Ari swept Sasha's knotted braids away from her face. "Were they mean to you?"

"What are you going to do about it? Bully them for making me feel bad?"

"I am your big sister," Ari said. "It would be well within my rights."

"Never mind," Sasha said. "It's in the past." Except she'd gone through the trouble of digging up the past, like an old smelly bone, for Nik who didn't even appreciate it. "So, Terrence is engaged…wow."

"He proposed to some woman in Hawaii. The photos were all over social media."

Sasha scoffed. "You mean he didn't ambush her at a party in front of all of their friends?"

"Maybe he's learned his lesson?" Ari proposed.

"Maybe…"

"Now that you know he's moved on, does that loosen the burden some?"

Sasha nodded. She wished him well.

"Good. It's time you stopped punishing yourself and cast off this curse."

She may not be cursed, but there was something wrong with her. Nik figured it out last night. What she cleverly packaged as "spontaneity" was in fact a toxic trait. She leaped into things without forethought and hoped for the best. When it turned out to be the worst, she bailed. That was something she'd have to work out on her own. Big sis couldn't come to the rescue.

Sasha slumped even deeper into the couch. "Thanks for putting up with me."

"I'm not putting up with you. I love you."

Ari slipped off her sandals and crossed her ankles on the coffee table next to the open laptop. She narrowed her eyes at it. Trick MacArthur's handsome face was frozen on the screen. "Stop giving this man views! You're only encouraging him."

"I thought you were over it," Sasha said.

"I was over it for like two days," Ari said.

"Now I'm back to being petty. I wish he'd go away."

"It's good to have you back," Sasha said with a chuckle. "We're the petty Witches of San Bernardino Valley."

"I can't stand to look at him."

Ari reached for the laptop and minimized the window of the website, only to reveal the expanded photo of Nik looking handsome and serious at Hillside Smokehouse displayed underneath. Sasha closed her eyes and could see him still, honey eyes, skin like molasses, glowing in the sun.

Ari gasped. "Where was this taken?"

"After the accident."

"Wait! You two were in an accident? When?"

"On the ride from the airport."

"Why didn't you mention it?"

"You would've freaked out, Mother Hen."

Already, Ari had gone pale underneath her peachy blush. "It sounds like the trip from hell. First the plane goes down. Then you're in a car accident."

"It was wild," Sasha said. "We survived it, though."

"Maybe you can survive this, too."

The last embers of hope flamed hot in Sasha's heart. She quickly stomped them out.

"Go take a shower," Ari said.

"You're obsessed with showers," Sasha observed. "Have you noticed that?"

"A hot shower can do wonders for your mental hygiene," she explained. "Now go. I'll clean up around here and make us lunch."

"Good luck with that. I don't have any food."

"Thank God for room service."

After a shower and lunch, Sasha sat at the table with her laptop, only this time she wasn't binge-watching the trickster's channel. She'd called for an emergency meeting with her therapist.

"Hello, Sasha," Dr. Jonas said in his usual reserved way. "Are things going well?"

"If they were, I wouldn't be calling, would I?"

"Therapy isn't solely for crisis management, you know."

"I'll keep that in mind."

"What's troubling you?"

"A lot has changed since we talked last." Sasha blinked fast to keep the tears at bay. "Nik and I are through."

Dr. Jonas nodded, absorbing the information. "I'm sorry to hear that."

"You said we were going too fast and—"

"I'm sorry to interrupt you, but I didn't say that."

"Yes, you did," she said sourly. She didn't think he was the type of person to backtrack on his clinical advice.

Dr. Jonas flipped open his notebook and checked his notes. "I asked if you were comfortable with pace and whether you questioned the timing. I pointed out that there were advantages to taking it slow."

Of course he had receipts.

"Here are some of the words you used to describe Nik." He slid his glasses further up his nose and started reading. "'He's perfect… He's wonderful'." Dr. Jonas shut the notebook. "Generally, when we use those types of words to describe a person or a situation, it's because we're not digging deep enough. No one and nothing is perfect, as you well know. You've chosen to perceive Nik as such. Call it a mirage. You're only seeing what you want to see."

"Well, he's not perfect, I can tell you that."

"Want to tell me what happened?"

She did her best recount the events. "I was trying to help, and he was so unappreciative."

"In trying to help," Dr. Jonas said tentatively, "you inadvertently put him in a difficult position at his workplace, which likely involved other colleagues."

Oliver was at that meeting, too. Sasha massaged her temples. "I understand that now."

"Where do you want to go from here?" Dr. Jonas asked.

"There's nowhere to go," Sasha said. "We're at an impasse. I kicked him out."

"I see."

"He accused me of hiding behind you and my sister, using you as a shield."

"Is that what you're doing?" Dr. Jonas asked.

"It feels that way..." Sasha admitted. "I don't want to rush into anything if it isn't right. Maybe this is a red flag that I was missing."

"He had a legitimate grievance," Dr. Jonas said. "Did he remain calm and respectful during the argument?"

Sasha looked down at her hands. There wouldn't have been an argument if it weren't for her. He'd wanted to walk away and cool down.

She wouldn't allow it. She was the one-woman red flag marching band.

"Do you have your journal?" Dr. Jonas asked.

She held up the leather-bound notebook.

"I want you to write a letter to your ex-fiancé to let him know how these last years have been, the ups and downs, all of it. Then ask him how he's doing."

She didn't have to ask. "I know how he's doing. I heard he—"

"No matter what you heard, you still don't know," Dr. Jonas said. "None of us knows what the other is going through."

Damn! He was good.

"Write the letter," he said. "See what comes up. Next time we'll talk about it."

Dear Terrence:

Did I ever say that I was sorry for what I'd done?

Not ending our engagement. I'm not sorry about that.

I'm sorry for entering the engagement, in the first place. I'm sorry for saying yes, for taking your ring. You were not the one for me. You didn't make me feel safe and respected. You didn't make me feel loved.

For years I lived under the shadow of your disappointment, your parents' disapproval and our mutual friends' rejection. I lived with the shame. I went so far as believing that something was inherently wrong with me, that I was cursed.

I'm done with all that, and I'm done with you.

Nonetheless, I send you love.

Your forever ex,
Sasha

Twenty-Three

Meet me at the trails at dawn.

Okay. That's just wishful thinking. Make that 7 AM.

Nik was at the diner where he'd ended up after a long, trying day at work. He'd told Oliver that he was no longer interested in pursuing Mad Dash, and was grateful when his friend had agreed.

"I didn't want to be the one to say it," he said. "But, yeah, let's ditch them. I'm more than happy to walk away—if there's even a deal to walk away from. We've heard nothing."

Once the decision was made, Nik put it out of his mind.

"Anyway, it's time you pivoted to Silicon Valley, don't you think?" Oliver asked. "That's the future."

"I'm not thinking about anything right now," he admitted. "It's all a freaking mess."

"Why are you even here?" Oliver asked. "Take the week off. Go work on things that matter to you."

That was code for Sasha; he knew it. She was the only thing that mattered to him at the moment. There was no deal he wanted to close, no future he wanted to imagine without her. They were running on four days without speaking, and Nik wasn't ashamed to admit that his life was crumbling.

The diner was the place he went to think. Ever since he brought Sasha there, it was filled with memories of her. He swore her laugh echoed off the walls. He was sitting at the same booth they had, eating pretty much the same meal, when the text messages popped up in quick succession. He stared at the phone in disbelief. Then he pushed back the stack of pancakes and called for the check.

He had somewhere to be bright and early in the early morning.

* * *

Nik was out of bed, dressed for a hike, and on his way to North Cove Park by dawn. He was antsy throughout the half-hour drive, his heart slamming in his chest. When he got there the parking lot was empty for a Friday morning. He welcomed the peace and the stillness. He hadn't yet worked out what he was going to say.

Then he saw the black SUV wind up the road. A moment later, it slid into the space next to the compact company car he drove while in Royal, and she stepped out.

Ariana shielded her eyes from the sun with a hand. The gesture brought back the image of Sasha standing to the side of the road after the accident. Sometimes, he didn't see the resemblance between them. Other times, like this, it was stunningly obvious.

"Good morning, Ariana."

He didn't dare call her "Ari" as she'd asked him to do on several occasions.

"Hello, Nik," she replied. "Let's walk."

They followed the same trail the three of them had taken in happier times. Ariana didn't say much. She walked with her head down, foregoing the large sunglasses she'd sported last time. Nik struggled with what to say, and the silence was as thin as the mountain air. Finally, he couldn't take it anymore.

"How is she?" he asked.

Ariana glared up at him. "She's a mess," she said. "Those are her words, not mine."

Nik's stomach flopped. The idea of her alone and unwell made him physically ill. "When was the last time you saw her?"

"Never mind that," Ariana said. "Have *you* tried to see her?"

"I don't think I'm welcome," he said. "She kicked me out."

Ariana nearly tripped. Nik caught her by the elbow just in time. She regained her balance and pushed forward. "I didn't know that."

"I was sure she was done with me," he said, after a while.

"Nah… She could've done worse."

"Like what?"

"Ask Ex what I put him through," Ariana said with a nervous laugh. "Better yet, don't! Let's focus on you."

"Here's the truth," Nik said. "I'd camp outside her door if I thought it made a difference. The thing is, I don't think she's sure about us."

"It hasn't been that long, you know," Ariana said. "Give her a chance to work up to that."

"We had one argument, and she stole the opportunity to blow us up."

"It's a defense mechanism. Sasha is more tenderhearted than most people realize. Honestly, you two met at the wrong time. She was still going through so much."

Nik refused to believe that. The circumstances that brought them together were unique and special, and could not be re-created. It wasn't as if he'd walked into a bar and picked her up. They'd crashed into each other's life.

"If you're worried she isn't over Terrence, don't be," Ariana said.

"She told you that?"

"She told me some of it. I can see where you're coming from, but I'm here today to tell you that you're wrong. Sasha was never into Terrence—that was the problem. That relationship should have died a natural death. Instead, Terrence resurrected it with a proposal. The breakup was messy. To this day, her sensitive heart couldn't handle the pain she'd caused. She's guilt-ridden. Rather than cling to myths like a family curse, she's come to terms that she's caused someone harm."

They arrived at the edge of a cliff overlooking the quarry. Ariana turned her back to the view. "Are you willing to fight for her?" she asked. "If you're not, let me know now. We'll never speak of this again."

Nik stared at the pink stone gleaming in the morning light. "All this time, I thought you didn't want us to be together."

"Come on, Nik. I saw the way she looked at you that first night, and I knew she was gone. All I wanted was for her to take her time and to see it, live it and believe in it. So, now I'm asking you, how do you feel about her?"

"I love her." This felt like the most natural thing in the world. It was a crime he still hadn't told her.

"Woah!" Ariana cried. "I wasn't expecting that!"

"I don't know what you were expecting," Nik said. "But I'm in love with her, and I'm a mess, too."

She grinned. "I don't have time to clean up these messes! In case you've forgotten, I've got a wedding to plan. So I have no choice but to get you two back together." She looped an arm around his and steered him back toward the trail. "Let's think of a plan."

Nik had been thinking of nothing else for days. "I'm way ahead of you, and I already have a plan."

"Good," Ariana said. "Now let's think of ways to make that plan even grander."

"You don't have to do that," Nik said.

"If this works out, I'm going to be your big sister, too," Ariana said.

"I believe I'm older than you."

"I don't care," Ariana said. "Get used to me bossing you around."

Twenty-Four

"We love the smokehouse submission!" Roxanne from *Table for Two* magazine exclaimed over the phone. "So much, we'd like to feature it in our July issue, rather than post it on our blog."

"That's exciting news!"

Sasha had stepped out of the stationery store to take the call. Ariana stayed behind assessing card stock and analyzing font sizes.

"We need to broaden our focus, step away from Michelin stars and celebrity chefs. Hillside Smokehouse has such a down-home quality, and your photos are incredible. One, in particular, would make an excellent cover."

"I'm on board, absolutely."

"Great. We've reached out to the owner and she's on board, as well."

Sasha loved a cover story as much as any journalist. For the moment, though, she'd take any assignment to keep busy. She hadn't heard from Nik since he'd walked out. The days without him were long and empty. The nights were wearing her down.

"We'll need additional photos," Roxanne said. "The barn is lovely, but it's not enough. We need to see the food, as well. We'll need a photo of Donna if she agrees to it, a few shots of tableware, the overall vibe of the restaurant and maybe a shot of your sister and her future husband enjoying the food."

"No."

It never failed. Everyone wanted a piece of Ari and Ex. If this were just a ploy to get the couple on the cover of the magazine, Sasha would turn it down.

"That's okay!" Roxanne said quickly.

"Are you still interested in running the story?" Sasha asked.

"Yes, of course! I had to ask. What kind of editor would I be if I hadn't?"

"Just so we're clear. The feature should be about Donna, not a celebrity couple."

"I agree. However, you of all people should understand the value of celebrity endorsement. Your sister could put Hillside Smokehouse on the map."

"The answer is still no," Sasha said. She refused to exploit family.

"Very well," Roxanne said. "Let's discuss deadlines. It's a short turnaround, so we'd have to move fast."

"That works for me. I'm in Texas for a limited time."

The sooner they got to work the better. As the wedding approached, she would have very little free time.

After she got off the phone with Roxanne, Sasha entered the boutique through a back door. They were no longer taking chances. The wedding planner arranged for private meetings for Ari with local shop owners. Ari was as paranoid as before. The less information Trick MacArthur could get his hands on, the better.

Ari was wrapping up her meeting with the calligrapher, a middle-aged man named Gerry with knotty fingers. Sasha browsed a display of stationery sets while she waited.

Late last night, it occurred to her that she ought

to write Nik a letter and apologize. She regretted the fight, and paid a high price for winning. She wasn't herself that night. Rather, she was a version of herself that she'd outgrown and was doing her best to leave behind. She wanted him to know that.

Nik was wonderful, but he wasn't perfect, and neither was she. Even so, he was the perfect partner for her.

Ari rose from the table. "We're done here. I'm pleased with my choice."

"That's good to hear," Dennis said. "We're grateful you chose us to fulfill your stationery needs, Ms. Ramos. It means a lot."

"You're welcome!" Ari said. "I'll make sure to post photos of my finished cards on social media and tag your shop."

Sasha couldn't help but think of Donna, and felt a twinge of guilt. She'd helped them out at a moment of need. Most people would not have stopped for total strangers.

"Ready to go?" Ari said.

"Hold on," she said. "I'd like to make a purchase."

Next, Ari had a meeting with Rylee, from which Sasha was blessedly excused. On the ride to the hotel to drop off Sasha, Ari asked about the work call. "How'd it go?"

"Great, actually," Sasha said. "I'd pitched a story to a culinary magazine. My photo might make the cover."

Ari squealed. "Another cover? Sasha, how awesome!"

"They need more photographs," Sasha said. "I'd have to get to work on it right away. I'll reach out to Donna and see when it's convenient to come out."

Ari went silent for a beat. "Is it the restaurant where you took that photo of Nik?"

Sasha stared out the window. It was a bright spring day in Royal. "The same."

"Interesting…"

"Why's that?" Sasha asked.

"No reason."

Ari pulled up to the hotel. The mirrored façade glistened in the sun. Sasha figured if she were going to ask, the time was now. "I wondered if you and Ex would like to help out?"

"What do you have in mind?"

"A photo of you and Ex having a romantic picnic on the grounds would break the internet and do wonders for a small business."

"You'd take the photos?"

"Of course. Who else?"

Ari nodded, as she tended to do when she was puzzling something out. "It would have to be soon. Ex's schedule is packed next week."

"That's fine with me," Sasha said. "I'll see what I can work out with Donna."

"Do that, and get in touch."

That went easier than Sasha had hoped. "Will do! Thanks for doing this."

"Are you kidding me?" Ari said. "A romantic photo shoot at a charming barn with my sister behind the camera? I wouldn't pass on that."

Sasha was glad she'd taken the chance and asked for the favor. Once alone in her suite, she took another chance. She sat at the table and wrote a note on the newly purchased stationery.

Nik,

You've tamed this wild heart. All I want is to come home.

I'm knocking. Let me in.

Sasha.

Twenty-Five

That bastard!

No sooner than Sasha left the note with Nik's doorman than she spotted him strolling home, looking smart in his usual suit, shirt collar open, no tie, phone pressed to one ear, and his free hand in his pocket. Chatting animatedly, laughing at times, the bastard didn't seem to have a care in the world.

Sasha's heart popped into a soggy mess, like a water balloon.

She flattened herself against the building across the street from his, hoping the wide-spreading branches of an oak tree would shield her from view. She checked the time. It was 6:30

p.m. on a Friday night. In all likelihood, he was returning home from the office. Maybe he'd stopped for drinks. Maybe he was on his way home to change and meet with whomever he was chatting with. Maybe he was on his way to dinner with someone new and exciting, another wild one caught in his net. Either way, he would get her note, read it and what…laugh?

Sasha broke into a cold sweat. What had possessed her to write those words, commit them to paper? *All I want is to come home? I'm knocking. Let me in.* Maybe she had hit her head in the accident. First thing, she would schedule a CAT scan.

It was too late to get the note back. Sasha had no choice but to stand there, helpless, and watch as he entered the building through the heavy glass doors. He paused midconversation to take the envelope from the doorman. Without a glance, he slid it in the inner pocket of his blazer and walked off.

The small voice of reason, which increasingly sounded like the voice of Dr. Jonas, whispered to her: *You're overreacting. This means nothing. He could be on the phone with his chiropractor or, more realistically, his cousin in Italy, for all you know.*

A sob cracked free from Sasha's throat. Soon a torrent of tears drowned out the voice of reason. Someone asked if she was okay. Clearly, she wasn't.

Sasha's feelings were validated the next morning. Nik hadn't reached out. He hadn't called or texted. He hadn't showed up at her door with flowers or written her a heartfelt note of his own. Her note was likely still in his jacket pocket, and the jacket on its way to the cleaners. Come to think of it, that was the best-case scenario.

Sasha sat up in bed and tossed aside her tear-stained pillow. Enough of this nonsense. She was the witch of San Bernardino Valley. The day she cried a man a river, he better drown in it.

She went into the bathroom, splashed cold water on her face and brushed her teeth with more aggression than any dentist would recommend. Then she ripped the silk scrunchie out of her hair and set her braids free. She was feeling like herself again.

First thing, she contacted Donna and scheduled the photo shoot. The only available date was Monday. "We're closed for business. It'll be easier that way."

"I agree."

With Ari and Ex making an appearance, it would be more discreet as well. They'd be able to roam around the property, unencumbered, like free-range chickens.

"Who knew that stopping to help you two lovebirds would get us featured in *Table for Two*?" Donna said in wonder. "Funny how life works."

Sasha did not have much to say. "Funny. Right?"

She'd obviously picked the wrong project to take her mind off Nik. That old barn was haunted with ghosts: their first meal together, their first real conversation, their first kiss in the parking lot… Everything was there. Donna called them lovebirds. It had felt that way to Sasha at the time. They'd had something. Where had it gone?

Thinking back, there were signs that things were waning. She'd attributed their falling-out to their blowout fight. Yet, he'd been avoiding her for days. He said he was preparing for the meeting, but who knew at this point? The way he'd bolted, eager to get away from her, after they'd had sex in her *kitchen,* of all places. Oh God!

There had been so many red flags that she'd simply chosen to ignore. Why was that? Because the man had helped her keep her cool during a flight? That made him a Good Samaritan or a good citizen, not a good boyfriend or life partner. There was a difference. He may deserve a medal, but he hadn't earned her heart.

Sasha closed her eyes and relived the scene:

Nik had reached over the middle passenger to tighten her seat belt and secure the oxygen mask over her nose. There was too much chaos for him to say anything. A child in the row behind them was wailing. He looked her in the eyes and let her know without a word that they were going to be okay, and she believed him. In that moment, she put all her trust in him. He was her hero.

It was time to move on from that fantasy.

After confirming the date and time with Ariana, Sasha sent an email to Roxanne to inform her that Hillside Smokehouse would indeed have the celebrity endorsement of Ariana Ramos and Xavier Noble. Her sister's only request was to not appear on the cover. "We don't want to grab the spotlight."

She spent the afternoon packing her gear. And then it was back to feeling despondent and depressed, as Nik did not call, text, show up with flowers or send a heartfelt note the entire weekend.

On Monday morning, they drove out to Hillside Smokehouse with Ex at the wheel. Three hours later, the navigation system instructed them to turn left onto a narrow road that Sasha knew well. Ari flipped up the car visor and gasped. “It’s beautiful!”

The old barn arose in the distance, its faded red paint bleeding into the ochre field. The beauty of the site hadn’t escaped her the first time around, which had prompted her to take those initial photos. This time, the sole purpose of her visit was to capture its silent grace, and her heart soared.

“I can’t believe I’ve never heard of this place,” Ex said. “Is the food any good, Sasha? Or is it all vibes?”

“Xavier!” Ari scolded.

“I’m just asking!” he said.

“The food is excellent,” Sasha assured him. “You won’t regret the drive.”

“We won’t regret it either way,” Ari said. “I want our wedding to draw attention to the beauty of the local community. This spot is darling.”

They pulled up to the front, bypassing the parking lot altogether. Donna came out to greet them. She looked fresh in a white eyelet dress. Her brown hair was pulled into a low ponytail to better reveal her startling blue eyes.

"You look beautiful!" Sasha cried.

"Sure," she said, "but no one's going to believe I cook in a fancy dress."

She had a point. "How about we start with shots of you in this dress out in the sunshine with the barn in the background. Then you can change into something else when we're in the kitchen."

Donna sighed in relief. "I'm so glad we're doing this with you."

"Thank you," Sasha said. "Allow me to introduce you to my sister, Ariana, and her fiancé, Xavier."

Donna welcomed them with warm hugs. "We're honored to have you here."

"Thanks for having us," Ari said.

"We've prepared a spread for you. Just a few snacks to get you through the day."

"You shouldn't have gone through the trouble," Ex said, in a tone that wasn't fooling anyone.

"It was no trouble at all."

"I'm going inside to set up," Sasha said. "I'll leave you two to get ready."

"Fine with us," Ex said, and made a beeline for the refreshments.

Sasha went into the kitchen, which looked nothing like the last time she was there. Donna's teenaged nephew, her appointed assistant for the day, asked if anything was wrong.

"It's too orderly," she replied. "Let's get some of the copper pots off the shelves and onto the counter."

"Yes, ma'am."

When they were done, she asked him to open some windows and shut others to better control the light. "This looks good," she said. "Let's see what the others are up to."

Ari and Ex were in the main dining hall, chatting with Donna. They'd changed into their first outfits. Ari looked stunning in a paisley dress and espadrilles. Her friend, Dee, had styled her for the occasion and she'd packed several outfit changes, even though the magazine had offered to supply a stylist.

Xavier looked striking in a fitted earthy brown suit, matching Stetson hat and boots. Sasha had no doubt the photo shoot was going to be epic.

They may not want to steal the spotlight, but there was no chance they wouldn't.

Donna left them to check in with her aging parents, the restaurant's original founders, who would also be featured in the shoot. Ex grabbed the chance to feed Ari a corn chip loaded with fresh guacamole. Sasha blindly grabbed her camera and took the shot.

The sound of the shutter startled Ari. "Hey! No fair! You didn't give us notice."

"Never mind me," Sasha said. "Just taking some candid shots, getting everyone used to the camera."

"Sure," Ari said. "Don't mind the woman with the telescopic lens."

The couple laughed, and Sasha kept right on snapping photos.

Moments later, Sasha asked her young assistant to take her to the site of the picnic.

"Actually," Ari said. "We changed our minds. No picnic."

"What?" Sasha cried. "I thought you liked the idea!"

"I *love* the idea," Ari said. "But I've been thinking: it's too similar to our engagement photo shoot in Italy. Also, it's too on the nose. Like we're trying to stage our love, and we're not. We'd like the photos to be more low-key and organic."

Says the woman throwing one of the most extravagant weddings ever, Sasha thought.

"Uh-oh," Ex said, still munching on chips and guacamole. "Sasha looks stressed."

"What do you expect? You're throwing me for a loop!"

"Settle down," Ari said. "Here's an idea. Ex and I will join Donna in the kitchen. She'll teach us a few recipes so we don't starve our first year of marriage. I don't know if you know this, but neither of us can cook."

"We're surviving on takeout," Ex added.

"Oh, I know," Sasha said.

"What do you think?" Ari asked.

Truthfully, the more she thought about it, the more she liked it. "It's not a bad idea."

"I'm a storyteller, Sasha!" Ari retorted. "I have good ideas."

"Does that mean I get to lose the hat?" Ex asked.

He was a Texan through and through, but cowboy hats and boots were not the author's style.

"Keep it for now," Sasha said. "You look good in it."

They started with a few photos of Donna and her family then Ex and Ari on the porch. Before they lost the light, they moved into the kitchen at which point Donna changed into her uniform and Ex ditched the hat, shrugged off the blazer and rolled up his sleeves.

Joining Donna in the kitchen turned out to be the absolute best idea Ari had ever had in her life. There was nothing staged about the shoot. Donna was at ease. She was happiest bossing people around in her kitchen and it showed. She walked Ari and Ex through the steps of a family recipe for chicken fried steak and several easy sides including the house favorite potato salad. They even whipped up dessert.

Sasha cleared her mind and got busy. If there were any ghosts lingering about, they'd left her alone for the day. She worked in peace, capturing all the fun, laughter and joy of cooking. Afterwards, they sat at a large wooden table to enjoy the meal. Sasha would never forget this day. Wasn't this the point of coming to Royal in the first place, to bond and make memories with her sister and her future husband?

Ari stepped out to take a call. When she returned, she nodded at Xavier. Sasha helped herself to a second serving of peach cobbler and pretended not to notice.

"Are we done for the day?" Donna asked. "Should I have the boys clear out the picnic setup?"

"Wait. There's a setup?" Sasha asked.

"Oh, yes," Donna replied. "A nice one, too, in the gazebo, using our fine china…collected at the local flea market, but still very fine."

Sasha set down her plate. "There's a gazebo on this property?"

"At the far end, near the orchard," she said. "It's a bit of a walk."

"I'd like to see it." Sasha got up from the table. "Anyone else?"

"Sorry. I'm stuffed," Ex said. "Take a photo."

Ari shook her head. "I'm exhausted. Cooking is hard work."

"I'd take you, but I need to clean up," Donna said.

"Just point the way. I'll find it."

"Follow me." Donna took her out the back door and pointed to a trail that curved around a bend. "You can't miss it."

"Would you be up to posing for photos at the gazebo later?" Sasha asked.

"We'll see how it goes." Donna pulled a cloth napkin from her apron pocket and dabbed at Sasha's chin. "Pardon me. You have a few crumbs."

"Thanks, Donna!"

"You're welcome."

Sasha switched her camera from one shoulder to the next, and slowly made her way down the path, kicking a stone along the way.

Watching Ari and Ex today made her realize that she wanted a love like theirs. It was inspiring to see them work together as a team, respectful of each other, yet always tender and attentive. She wanted a relationship like that, a true partnership with someone who would enhance her life. Sasha had thought that person might be Nik. Even though it hurt her heart to accept this, it was clear he wasn't the one for her. Yet she had hope. Her mother and grandmother had gotten over their pasts and found love and happiness. So could she.

The gazebo came into view in the distance. The white iron structure was softened with green vines. Sasha had to snap a photo. It was too beautiful. Not just the gazebo itself, but the path leading up to it and the cluster of trees beyond. She raised the camera to her eye and adjusted the lens. She framed the image and there he was.

Nik was on the step, looking incredible in jeans and a black T-shirt, a bouquet of white tulips in his hand.

Sasha dropped the camera. Considering that it cost over two thousand dollars, she was thankful that it was secure with a strap. She took a few steps forward, shrinking the distance between them. He was looking at her with those soft honey eyes. She steeled herself against their charms.

"What are you doing here?" she asked.

"Waiting for you."

"Is that right?"

He took a step down. "Can we talk, please?"

"What is there to talk about?" she demanded. "You think you can just show up, looking incredible, and sweep me off my feet?"

"That was the plan," Nik admitted. "Not the looking incredible part. I'm hoping to look lost and sorry."

"Ha!" Sasha spat. "You're not lost. I saw you the other night. You looked as happy as ever."

Nik lowered the flowers onto the step and took a few careful steps toward her.

"You don't have to tiptoe," she said. "I'm not a wild cat. I won't run away."

"Fair enough," he said, and closed the distance between them. The fresh scent of his cologne instantly enveloped her. "I don't understand what you're saying. Where did you see me? I haven't been anywhere."

"The night I dropped off the note," she said.

"Friday?"

"Yes, Friday." This only confirmed that he'd read it. Not responding in any way was a choice.

"I'm confused, Sasha. I worked late, went straight home and ordered in. Where could you have possibly seen me?"

"On your street," she replied. "I'd just left the note with your doorman and saw you walking home. You were on the phone, laughing, as if you didn't have a care in the world. Meanwhile I…"

Sasha could not continue. She'd sooner die than admit that she stood on the sidewalk bawling her eyes out for a good quarter hour.

"Oh, Sasha…" His desire to reach out to her was plain in his eyes. She would not let him. Sasha wanted answers. If he'd showed up at her door on Friday night with those same tulips, she would have thrown herself at him, but she was not that person anymore. With each passing day, she was growing into a stronger version of herself.

Nik pulled out his phone and started scrolling. When he found what he was looking for, he smiled. "Would you say it was around six thirty Friday evening?"

She shrugged. It was six thirty on the dot, but she was keeping her cards close to her chest.

He handed her the phone, opened to a call log.

Friday 4:10 PM UNKNOWN NUMBER SCAM LIKELY [MISSED CALL]

Friday 6:23 PM ARIANA RAMOS

"Ari called you?"

It made perfect sense. Someone had tipped him off and told him where to find her today. They were all in on this, even Donna! This picnic at the gazebo was a trap.

"We went hiking Friday morning, just the two of us."

Now Sasha was dumbfounded. "Are you like friends now?"

"We're co-conspirators," he said. "I wasn't sure

you ever wanted to see me again. Your sister reached out and gave me hope."

Wait one second!

"*I* gave you hope, Nik!" She sounded unhinged, but couldn't stop herself. "Every word of that note was to give you hope. Didn't you read it?"

"Of course I read it."

"And you thought showing up with flowers three days later was the appropriate response?"

"If you think it was easy for me to sit back and wait, then you don't know me very well."

Sasha handed him his phone. "Make me understand."

The voice of reason was back, questioning why she was pushing it? This was literally everything she'd wanted. She ought to rush into his arms and be done with it. Yet she couldn't.

"I was on the phone when the doorman gave me your note," Nik said. "He didn't say who it was from, and frankly I didn't bother to ask. Your sister and I were plotting and scheming, figuring out a way to get you to this very gazebo. I only read it last night, and by then it was too late. I thought it was best to wait."

Nik hesitated and reached for her hand. "It was my plan to bring you out here all along. I had no idea how to go about it, outside hiring someone to kidnap you. On Friday night, your sister called with news about the photo shoot. I was so proud of you for getting that job, by the way. You're so talented. I would've loved to see you at work."

Sasha could've kissed him then, but held strong. "Thanks," she said. "Go on."

"If I was laughing that night, if I seemed happy at all, it's because everything was falling into place. I was grateful for the chance to tell you how I feel at the very place where I fell in love with you."

That did it. Sasha bolted into his arms. He caught her, and they stumbled together into a bed of grass.

"I love you." Sasha cupped his face and spoke the words into his kiss.

Nik rolled her onto her back and pinned her down. "My wild one…" he said. "I'm the one who desperately wants to come home. I'm sorry I got upset over something so trivial. I could've lost you."

"That's impossible," Sasha said. "I caught you that first day, and you're mine."

"What a lucky day that was!"

She laughed. "That's a bit of revisionist history."

"Honey, I want a future with you," he said. "A life full of adventure."

"So do I," Sasha whispered. She wanted it with all her heart.

"This conversation may be premature, but I promise never to ask you to marry me," he said. "I won't put you in that position again."

Sasha raised her chin, defiant. "What if I asked you?"

Nik pulled away and spoiled her with the most devilish grin. "What if you asked for my hand in marriage, you mean?"

"Yes, Nik. Could you handle that?"

"Sasha, you've cursed me to a life of loving you. How could I ever say no?"

* * * * *